THE NEGRO QUESTION WHO AM I

COPYRIGHT 2011 BY LEE CUMMINGS

ALL RIGHTS RESERVED, NO PART OF T
REPRODUCED OR TRANSMITTED IN AI
MEANS WITHOUT WRITTEN PERMISSI(

ISBN-9781097362981

AUTHOR LEE CUMMINGS

Who am I?

When you are through reading this book you will know the truth about yourself! This book traces **the footsteps of the Negro in the Americas and Caribbean backwards** in time to the land of the black headed people....**Mesopotamia.** There was a man born in the land of the black headed people who was called Abraham and **there is a true image of this black Abraham in this book that is 2300 years old.** This book traces the offspring of Abraham **from Mesopotamia** to the land of Canaan **(North Africa)** to the Kingdom of Judah **(Slave Coast-West Africa)** to the Americas. **You will see official maps that were created for the kings of France and England that called the original name of the Slave Coast...The Kingdom of Judah.** This book proves that the Kingdom of Judah (Slave Coast) was sold into the North Atlantic Slave trade and ended up in the Americas and the Caribbean. We will trace the footsteps of the black Jews from the slave plantations in the South to the ghettos of the North. This book provides the reader with **eyewitness accounts that the original colonists of the 13 colonies were black people.** This book relies on the testimony of the great American, Benjamin Franklin, who states that America, France, Russia, Italy, Sweden, Spain and Germany were black nations in 1751.**This book is revised, restructured and free of typos.** I have updated the timelines, images and the construction of this book...love you!

TABLE OF CONTENTS

CHAPTER 1: BLACK BUT NOT AFRICAN   PAGE 4

CHAPTER 2: ISRAELITE COLONIES   PAGE 23

CHAPTER 3: ISRAEL IN WEST AFRICA   PAGE 28

CHAPTER 4: THE SHIPS OF BABEL   PAGE 53

CHAPTER 5: THE NEGRO RESISTANCE   PAGE 65

CHAPTER 6: THE 13 BLACK BRITISH COLONIES   PAGE 106

CHAPTER 7: BLACK TROOPS OCCUPY THE 13 COLONIES   PAGE 114

CHAPTER 8: THE QUARREL OF THE COVENANT   PAGE 130

CHAPTER 9: IF IT BE A SON KILL HIM   PAGE 153

CHAPTER 10: THE UNTHINKABLE   PAGE 163

CHAPTER 11: THE MORNING TRAIN   PAGE 174

CHAPTER 12: WAR WITH THE GOD OF ISRAEL   PAGE 186

CHAPTER 13: THE ANSWER TO THE NEGRO QUESTION   PAGE 197

CHAPTER 14: THE WHITE JEWISH QUESTION   PAGE 200

CHAPTER 15: THE EUROPEAN SECRET   PAGE 214

CONCLUSION   PAGE 229

CHAPTER 1   BLACK BUT NOT AFRICAN!

IMAGE-PALACE OF ZIMRI LIN-ORIENTAL MUSEUM-CHICAGO ILL
THIS IMAGE IS 5000 YEARS OLD

Ever since the so called Negro came into contact with the European's through the slave trade, there have been a number of legitimate questions concerning this Negro. Number (1) which of the son's of Noah is his father? Number (2) where did the Negro have his origination? Number (3) is he African or Mesopotamian? Number (4) who is the Negro in America? In order to understand who this so-called Negro is we must first begin this book with examining this picture found in Amari, (northwest Sumer). The brown skinned people in the picture happen to be the ancient Sumerians. This image from the Palace of Zimri Lin shows black people in Mesopotamia.....**5000 years ago!**

The blackest man to the far right of the image on page 4 is not a Mesopotamian...in the book of Acts (Acts 2:9 &10) he was known as a Libyan but in our generation he is called an African! Even though the Mesopotamian and the African are black, they are different people. The ancient Mesopotamians were a black people from ancient times and they are still black today....even though most of them have forgotten their true history. All of the Nations have been moving from Nation to Nation since the Lord scattered the Nations at the tower of Babel. The white European is in Africa, America and Australia. The Ottoman Turk has landed in Arabia and swears up and down that he is the original Arabian even though the artifacts disagree with him. What is lacking in this World today? Good teaching....the school system has failed and so has the Church....we are men most miserable.

SARGON THE GREAT
BRITISH MUSEUM
3500 YR OLD IMAGE

ABRAHAM SLAYING ISAAC
LATINA CATACOMB
ROME -320 A.D

Abraham the Mesopotamian was a black man and so were his descendants. The image of Abraham to the right depicts him and Isaac as being black. The image is at least seventeen hundred years old! The bust on the left is that of Sargon the great, a Sumerian tablet was found that was written by Sargon. The tablet said," I Sargon rule over the back headed people of Sumer." In the tablets of Sumer the ancient Sumerians described themselves as the black headed people. The ancient Sumerians were a people from Mesopotamia...they were black (still black) but not African. We have been programmed in America with **the phrase," all blacks come from Africa,"** this phrase has become a stumbling block to the elders and the so-called scholars of this World!

ELAMITE WARRIORS AND MODERN MESOPOTAMIANS

ELAMITE WARRIOR-BRITISH MUSEUM SEED OF ABRAHAM-MESOPOTAMIA	MODERN IRAQ'S GOOGLE

BRITISH MUSEUM	BRITISH MUSEUM	BRITISH MUSEUM
KING SHULGI	KING GUDEA	SARGON

The ancient people of Mesopotamia were clearly black people but they were not African! These three black kings; King Shulgi of Ur, King Gudea of Lagash and King Sargon of Accad, were all Mesopotamian Kings, yet neither of these three black kings are the sons of Africa (Ham). In fact, Sargon the Great ruled from Elam to the Mediterranean Sea. The education that we received in the United States was designed to make sure that the so-called Negro would never know that he ruled Europe and the whole World at one time! **This book proves that.**

The People of Mesopotamia, Iraq and Iran still retain their blackness. The Zondervan **Pictorial bible dictionary (page 330) states that Ham is the progenitor of Mizraim, Cush, Put, and Canaan but not the Negro!** As you can see Mesopotamia was inhabited by black somewhat baldheaded people. This fact is of extreme importance when weighed on a scale with the evidence that I shall present. **And so Abraham, the black Mesopotamian leaves Ur of Sumer (SHINAR) and heads into the land of Canaan,** Genesis (Genesis 11:31, 32) and Genesis 12:5. Subsequently, Abraham has a son by the name of Isaac who in turn has a son by the name of Jacob. **Remember that Abraham is a black man from Mesopotamia and his sons look like him.** I have the artifacts that prove Abraham was a black man. Let's proceed to the life of Jacob it is written in 1st Chronicles **(1st Chronicles 2:1 & 2)** that Jacob, Israel, had twelve sons; Rueben, Simeon, Levi, Judah, Issachar, Zebulon, Dan, Joseph, Benjamin, Naphtali, Gad and Asher. On the next page are images of the Egyptian King Tut and Queen Nefeteri. **Abraham the black Mesopotamian travels into the land of Canaan; 2119B.C.**

MODERN EGYPTIANS LOOK LIKE THE ARTIFACTS

**QUEEN NEFETERI
BRITISH MUSEUM**

**KING TUT
BRITISH MUSEUM**

MODERN EGYPTIANS GOOGLE-BLACK EGYPTIANS

The Egyptians were and still are a black people until this very day....contrary to what some fanciful European writer has written. If you said they these black Egyptians don't look like the Arabs in Egypt today you are correct. The white Arabs in Egypt today are the descendants of the Ottoman Turk Empire. When the Ottoman Turks invaded Arabia **(1517 A.D)** they displaced the black Arabians and placed the white Turkish population all over Arabia.....this is a historical fact! In case you weren't aware of this....**the name Egypt means black.**

Let's visit a scene in the book of Genesis where Jacob is dying. In Genesis 47:28- 31 Jacob dies, then in Genesis 50:7 – 11, all of Jacobs 12 sons and the princes of Egypt go up to bury Jacob. waiting in the wings are the Canaanites who for some odd reason think that everybody in the funeral procession is an Egyptian and do you know why? It is because everyone at the funeral was black!

QUEEN NEFETERI SEED OF HAM BRITISH MUSEUM	ELAMITE WARRIOR SEED OF SHEM BRITISH MUSEUM	HAGAB-JUDEAN SEED OF SHEM ISRAEL MUSEUM

As you can clearly see, the seed of Ham and Shem have black skin but they have different fathers! Shem is the father of the **Mesopotamians (Hebrew Israelites)** and the so-called Negro in the Americas'; Ham is the father of the Africans/Libyans. The white Europeans to this very day think that the African and the so-called Negro is of the same lineage and why? Because we are both a black skinned people but when your eyes become trained you can see the difference....it is like night and day. The seed of Ham/African is extremely black with high cheek bones; he shares the same cheekbone structure with his brother the Chinese! If you don't believe that the **Chinese are direct descendants** of the black African see the B.B.C news article concerning the subject; Chinese geneticist discover genetic link to Africa.

Even though the three black persons on page 10 look alike, they are not of the same lineage. Nefeteri is from Ham's seed, the Elamite warrior or Mesopotamian is from Shem's seed. The Judean archer (Hagab) is also descended from Shem's seed (the tribe of Judah). Don't forget that Abraham, Isaac and Jacob are descended from Shem. Of importance, this Nefertiti would be considered a Negro by today's use of the word. Lastly, there is an image of Joseph the son of Jacob wearing an Egyptian garb. Joseph was sold into Egyptian bondage in 1926 B.C; **Jacob Israel, the Mesopotamian, went down into Egypt with his sons and grandchildren in 1904 B.C.**

JOSEPH THE SON OF JACOB-COIN-MUSEUM CAIRO EGYPT
COIN READS-JOSEPH THE VICEROY OF EGYPT-COIN AGE-3900 YRS

As you can see, based on the coins image.... Joseph of the Bible was a black man. Whoever you are on the other side of this book....we have been taught lies and for what reason? The idea was to make you forget that the original Mesopotamians were a black race of people. So **they came up with the phrase," all blacks come from Africa."** They knew that once you figured out Abraham came from ancient black Mesopotamia...you would figure out that Abraham was a black man indeed! Once you came into this simple truth then the dominos would start falling into place....Abraham's seed; Isaac, Jacob and the 12 tribes would have to be black. This is what they fear the most...you finding out that you are Israel. The Negro Question book series proves that without anger or prejudice.

ABRAHAM AND ISAAC-DURA EUROPA SYNAGOGUE-2300 YR OLD IMAGE

This is an image of the black Hebrew Abraham attempting to sacrifice his black son Isaac as the other black Hebrews look on! This image was located in Syria and do you know why? Antiochus Epiphany deported the black Jews here in 168 B.C! Let's turn our attention back to Joseph, the son of Jacob.

ARTICLE:

An Egyptian paper claims that archaeologists have discovered ancient Egyptian coins bearing the name and image of the Biblical Joseph.

The report in Al-Ahram boasts that the find backs up the Koran's claim that coins were used in Egypt during Joseph's period. Joseph, son of the Patriarch Jacob, died around 1450 B.C.E., according to Jewish sources. These Jewish scholars are wrong and their timeline is off by 383 years. **Joseph was born in 1943 B.C** and was made Governor **(12th Dynasty of Egypt)** over all Egypt **during the reign of Pharaoh's; Sensuret 2 and Amenhetet 2; Joseph died in 1833 B.C. at the ripe old age of 110 years. See the Negro Question part 5 Joseph and the 12th dynasty of Egypt; all of the research can be found in the Negro Question Part 5.** Excerpts from the Al-Ahram report, as translated by Mideast Media:"In an unprecedented find, a group of Egyptian researchers and archaeologists have discovered a cache of coins from the time of the Pharaohs. Its importance lies in the fact that it provides decisive scientific evidence disproving the claim by some historians that the ancient Egyptians were unfamiliar with coins and conducted their trade through barter."The researchers discovered the coins when they sifted through thousands of small archaeological artifacts stored in the vaults of the Museum of Egypt. Initially they took them for charms, but a thorough examination revealed that the coins bore the year in which they were minted and their value, or effigies of the pharaohs who ruled at the time of their minting. **Some of the coins are from the time when Joseph lived in Egypt, and bear his name and portrait.** So far, it should be obvious to you that the Mesopotamians, Egyptians and Hebrews are a black people....nothing has changed. Let's look at Moses, the seed of Shem, and see if he was also mistaken for an Egyptian. There is an interesting story in Exodus **(Exodus 2:16-19)** about a man named Jethro who had 7 daughters; one day when they went to water the livestock they were being harassed and Moses helped them. When the women came home, the old man Jethro asked them why were they home so early and they said," **an Egyptian helped us.**" The Egyptian that they were referring to was none other than Moses....the Hebrew Israelite!

MOSES-DURA EUROPA SYNAGOGUE-2300 YR OLD IMAGE

This image of Moses was recovered from the Dura Europa

Synagogue in Syria; this image is 2300 years old and depicts the **Levite Moses as a black man!** Let's see if this is a reoccurring theme with the seed of Shem being mistaken for an Egyptian. Let's run down to the book of Acts and ear hustle **(listen in on)** on a conversation a Roman soldier is having with the Apostle Paul. See Acts (Acts 21:37-40). The Roman soldier asked Paul if he was that Egyptian who led 400 men into the wilderness but Paul's response was," I am a Jew." Paul was mistaken for a black Egyptian. In **Romans 11:1 Paul is specific and tells the reader that he is from the tribe of Benjamin!** I have placed an image of the black Benjamite King Saul on this page so that you can see what a Benjamite actually looked like!

KING SAUL-THE BENJAMITE
BRISTOL PSALTER, BRITISH LIBRARY-LONDON-1000 YRS OLD!

This is what the tribe of Benjamin looked like and you can't say that I am prejudiced because this image comes out of London. This is the first time that we have seen an image of King Saul the Benjamite! **This is what Paul looked like.**

If **Ham is not the Negros father** and **Japheth is not the Negros father**....Thru the process of elimination the Negros father must be Shem! We know that Shem is the father of the Israelites of the Bible and therefore the so-called Negro must be Israel! I shall proceed to show you how the black Mesopotamians or Hebrew Israelites made their way to the west coast of Africa. There were 5 incidents that proceeded to push the black Israelites into the interior of Africa; (1) the ancient black Assyrians invaded Israel **in** 722 B.C (**2 Kings 17th chapter**) and deported ten of the tribes to Assyria. If you pay attention to wars in this generation when Nations are invaded the people flee to the neighboring Nation to avoid war and in the case of the Assyrian Invasion, the Hebrews fled to the interior of Africa and I shall prove this! **The Hebrew Israelites fled into Africa (took refuge)** during the **Babylonian invasion in 606 B.C**, the **Roman invasion in 70 A.D**, the **Arab invasion in 640 A.D** and a subsequent **Roman invasion in 132 A.D**. In 132 A.D Hadrian Caesar destroyed Jerusalem and forbade the Jews from entering the gates of the city. When Jesus/YHSW was born Joseph and Mary fled to Egypt to avoid an assassination attempt on his life by King Herod. **Jesus had hair like lamb's wool** and **his feet looked as though it was burned in a furnace** (Revelation 1:9-12). This is the reason **the black Royal family;** Joseph-Prince of Judah, Mary-Judean Princess and Jesus-heir to the throne of David fled to Egypt....they were black just like the Egyptians!

Africa/Libya has long been a place of safety for the black Hebrews when fleeing advancing armies. Is there any proof in the Bible to validate **(prove)** such a boastful claim by the writer? Let's turn to the book of Acts and see what the Holy Ghost had the Apostle Peter to tell the congregation where Israel was residing! See the book of Acts **(Acts 2:8-10).** These verses state that Jews from every nation under heaven came up to Jerusalem to keep Pentecost and specifically mention Cyrene and Libya; **Libya is the ancient name for Africa**. Libya was the ancient name of Africa, go back and read your history books, the Lord had Peter to write that Israel not only resided in Africa but that Israelite children had been born in the land of Africa! I have provided a map for you on the next page of this book that proves the ancient name of Africa was none other than Libya. Few ministers are aware of this fact.... that the Apostle Peter is giving the World order in his generation and yet....no one believes his report. **SEE THE NEXT PAGE.**

STRABO MAP- 20 A.D, GOOGLE MAPS

This is what the World knew to be true during the times of Jesus/YSHW; Jesus would have been 26 years old at the time that this map was created by the Greek Cartographer Strabo. **Libya is the name of the continent that this generation calls Africa.** If you will allow the testimony of the Apostle Peter into this discussion, he will tell you the location of the children of Israel in 30 A.D. Grab your Bible and turn to Acts 2:9 & 10 and you will see that **the Hebrew Israelites were living all over the Earth;** Libya/Africa, Asia and Europe. Israel fled into West Africa when fleeing alien armies. **This will become important when you visit the data on the 13 black British colonies.**

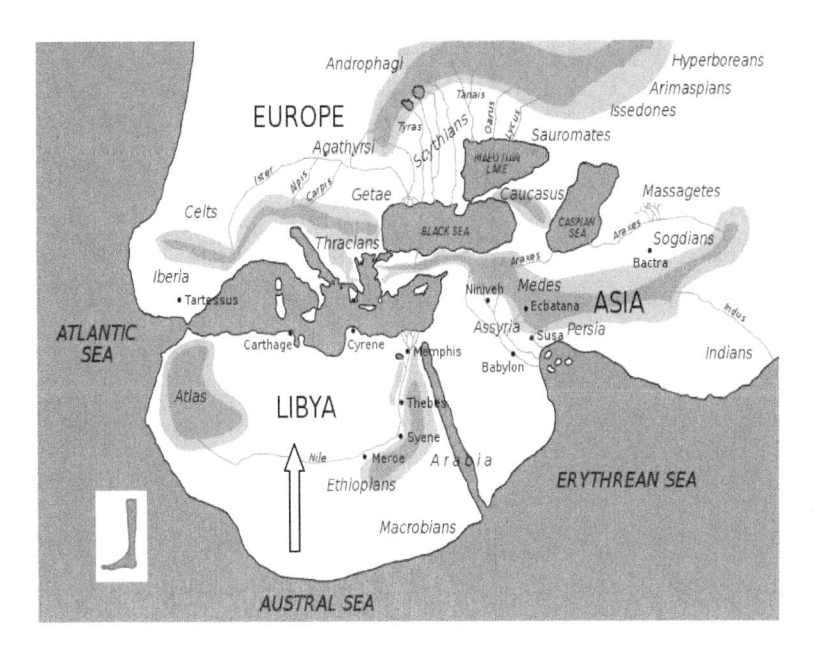

**MAP OF HECATAEUS-550 B.C
GOOGLE MAPS**

Even in the days of the Apostle Peter, Israel had mingled himself among the sons of Ham; before I precede any further I shall provide you with further proof that Israel had no problem living among the sons of Ham. See Ezra the 9th chapter, verses 1 and 2; it states that Israel had mingled among the Canaanites, Hittites, Perizittes, Jebusites, Ammonites, Moabites, Egyptians, and the Amorites. These are all the black tribes or black sons of Ham. You can find them listed as Ham's sons in the Tenth chapter of Genesis. Now for the question of the last 2000 years where is the proof that Israel is among the African nations? **It's interesting that the new translations of the Bible don't give this basic understanding and in fact nor do the schools of**

Seminary....can this be mere coincidence or is this part of a bigger cover-up? According to the last census taken by the U.S Government there are currently 42 million blacks in America....that is an increase of 22 million blacks since 1960! Think for a moment, not only have children been born to the Negro in this captivity, the Negro has also created children with women of other races. The black man in America has married the Japanese, Pekinese, Chinese, white Europeans and basically every race of women he has come in contact with and yet... His skin color hasn't changed in 6000 years! Below is an image of a group of Mesopotamian black men and African black men, can you tell the difference?

TOMB OF BENI HASAN-EGYPT-18TH DYNASTY

In the top fresco the Egyptians are beating the Hebrew Israelite who is on his knees; **in the bottom fresco the Egyptians have on white garments,** the other men are black Hebrew Israelites.

If I had not told you who these men were you never would have guessed it in a million years! This is the problem that the North Atlantic slave trade presents to the so-called historian in this current generation. **The black Jews fled into West Africa fleeing the Assyrians in 722 B.C, when fleeing the Babylonians in 606 B.C, when fleeing the Romans in 70 A.D and when fleeing the Arabs in 640 A.D.** Look at the center of the map below....**the slave coast was called the kingdom of Judah.**

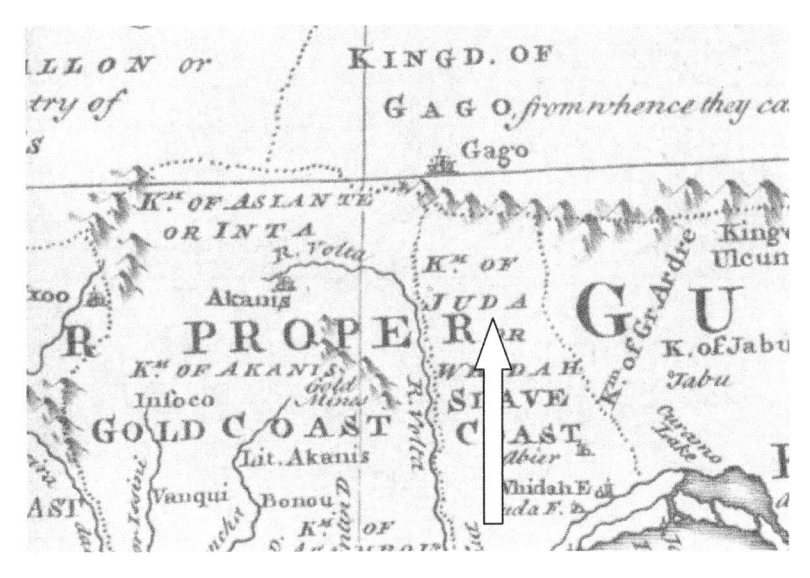

MAP-AN ACCURATE DESCRIPTION OF NEGRO LAND-1747
CARTOGRAPHER-EMANUEL BOWEN
MAP LOCATION - NORTHWESTERN UNIVERSITY-EVANSTON ILL

This map was created by Emanuel Bowen; cartographer to King Louis the 15th of France and King George the 2nd of England. This map was created in 1747 and gives the original name of the Slave Coast ....as the Kingdom of Judah!

I have identified three tribes that came into the Americas via the North Atlantic slave trade; Judah, Levi and Benjamin. You have been walking thru the Americas thinking you were an African American....well you aren't...you are the Jew of the Bible and I have further proof. There was a Hebrew colony at Carthage and its leader was a black Phoenician named Hannibal!

**HANNIBAL OF CARTHAGE
WILDWIND COINS**

SHYQL YSHRAL-YR 1

The ancient Phoenicians founded Carthage in 814 BC but what the historians fail to tell us is that the Phoenicians were Hebrew Israelites and their alphabet proves it.

This is the alphabet of the black Phoenicians and it is identical to the alphabet of the ancient Jews. In Hebrew/Phoenician the coin actually reads; SHQL YSHRAL, ALAPH OR YAR 1. This coin is referencing the 1st Jewish revolt against Rome in 70 A.D. **Ancient Carthage was in North Africa.**

CHAPTER 2   **ISRAELITE COLONIES**

Carthage (AFRICA) was a Jewish colony founded in North Africa in the year 800 B.C by the black Phoenicians. It could have been a place of refuge for the Israelites fleeing the Assyrian invasion of 722 B.C; **See 2ndKings Chapter 17**. The black Carthaginians and General Hannibal were defeated by the Romans in 201 B.C; the Romans were led by the Roman General Scipio Africanus. The Romans defeated the black Hebrews of Carthage and the name Africanus began to be spread all over Libya. This is where the name Africa has its origination.

**THE PHOENICIAN CADMUS FIGHTING THE DRAGON-689 B.C
LOUVRE MUSEUM-PARIS FRANCE**

This coin is that of the black Carthaginian, **Cadmus,** he is responsible for giving the Hebrew Alphabet to the Greeks. Phoenicia was located in North Africa; this black Jew was from Africa. Remember... **the Egyptian foot** represents the footsteps that the seed of Abraham took from Mesopotamia into Africa.

I have located a seal that has been written with the Paleo Hebrew Alphabet. This seal belonged to King Jeroboam of Israel. See the seal below.

SEAL DATED TO 980 B.C
ROCKEFELLER MUSEUM, JERUSALEM

Carthage was located in North Africa and it is evident from the Alphabet that these people were descended from the Jews of the Bible and they were black! Ancient Carthage, Tyre and Sidon were Phoenician states and are mentioned in the Bible. In fact one of the Phoenician States had a city in it called Zara-Phath or Zara faith. Zarah was one of the sons of Judah and King James...the one that translated your Bible ...claims descent from Zarah. Let's get back to the black Jewish colonies in Africa.

Cyrene (Africa) not much is known of Cyrene but we do know black Jews were born there, according to the Apostle Peter in the 2nd chapter of Acts **(Acts 2:10).** Some of the prophets and teachers came from there according to Acts 13:1 and they were black...how do I know this? One of the prophets...**Simeon was called Niger**...in ancient times if you were extremely black you were called Niger. The close proximity to the Nile River would make fleeing into Africa a quick exit from an invading army. History has recorded that the **Cyrenaica Jews revolted in 115 A.D under the Romans,** and that it ceased to exist after the Arab invasion in 640 A.D.

Alexandria Africa; history states that **the black Jews of Alexandria** were present with the founding of this city by Alexander the Great in 332 B.C. History also records that the city was wiped out by the Roman's during the Jewish revolt in 115 A.D to 117 A.D.

Elephantine (Africa): as late as 494 B.C documents show that this Jewish community had a temple at Elephantine; there was a temple to YHWH (JEHOVAH) and that some of the people were soldiers.

Memphis (Africa); it is a Biblical fact that Jeremiah the Prophet and the kings seed sought refuge in Egypt (which is in Africa). See the book of Jeremiah (**Jeremiah 44:1-8**) **Verse 1,** The word of the Lord that came to Jeremiah <u>**concerning all the Jews which dwell in the land of Egypt**</u>, which dwell at Migdol, and at Tahpanhes and at Noph, and in the country of Pathos saying. **Verse 8,** In that ye provoke me unto wrath with the works of your hands burning incense unto other <u>**gods in the land of Egypt wither ye be gone to dwell!**</u> This is the testimony of the Most High God himself...**God is telling you out of his own mouth that Israel had fled into Africa; Egypt is in Africa/Libya.** Judah had been invaded by the Babylonians under King Nebuchadnezzar between 606 B.C and 587 B.C.... according to <u>**your King James Bible**</u>....Jeremiah and the few Jews that remained voted and returned to Egypt. In case you are wondering why **this Egyptian Hieroglyphic (Foot) keeps showing up in this book,** it has been placed here to show the travels of the black Mesopotamian; who became the black Hebrew Israelite and who in turn became the Negro.

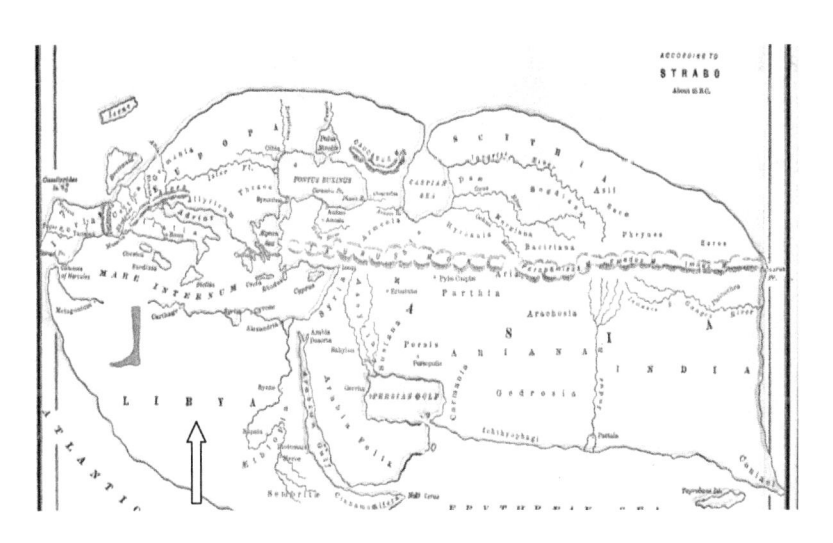

LYBIA THE ANCIENT NAME OF AFRICA

STRABO MAP-GOOGLE MAPS 20 A.D

Let's do a brief recap on what we have learned so far. We have proven that Abraham was a black Mesopotamian and that the ancient Mesopotamians were a black race of people. We proved that the Hebrew Israelites fled into Africa/Libya every time their homeland was invaded; Assyrian invasion-722B.C, Babylonian invasion-606 B.C, Roman invasion-70 A.D, Arab invasion-640 A.D and another Roman invasion in 132 A.D. We proved that there were Jewish colonies all over Africa. Before I leave this chapter I just remembered that when Abraham left Ur of the Chaldeans he and Sarah went to live in Egypt. **See Genesis 12:10;** Abraham had his first born son by an Egyptian woman by the name of Hagar. This union produced the Arabs or the Arabians and the religion Islam!

CHAPTER 3   ISRAEL IN WEST AFRICA

When Joshua is handing out the inheritance to the children of Israel he begins to give Judah his inheritance, see Joshua the 15th chapter beginning with verse 20-42, emphasis on verse 42; **to the tribe of Judah was given the city Ashan.** Next run to Joshua (Joshua19:1-7) verse 1, to Simeon was given an inheritance. Verse 7, in **Ashan**. Next, let's examine **1st Chronicles 6:50-59;** to the Levite was given an inheritance in **Ashan** with her suburbs. So we have 3 tribes mentioned in the bible whose dwelling was in Ashan, in the land of Judah. There was a tribe located in west Nigeria called **the Ashanti, the ti means the people of**. The Ashanti Empire fought wars against the British Empire and won some and lost some. The Ashanti were situated next door to the Kingdom of Judah in West Africa; near the Slave Coast and gold coast. This is that which was spoken of by the prophet Jacob when he was dying; see Genesis **(Genesis 49:8-10)** verse 10, **the scepter shall not depart from Judah or the law giver from between his feet.** Judah holds the scepter and Levi is the teacher of the law...hence Jesus (Prince of Judah) and John the Baptist (Levite).These two tribes must always remain together....whether free or captive!

MAP OF ASHANTI EMPIRE- GOOGLE MAPS

The Ashanti/Levites fought five wars against the British known as the Anglo Ashanti wars. These wars were fought between the Years 1823 and 1900.....on the Worlds time line that was yesterday! In any war in which the Ashanti lost the men were deported into the Americas specifically Jamaica. These Ashanti or Levites would later be known to the world as Jamaicans!

Below is a picture taken from the London times, in the year 1848, by Sir Henry M Stanley. **This picture shows an Ashanti priest crossing the Prah River in Nigeria** with a cap on his head, which reads holy to YHWH, **and** a breastplate on his chest with 12 stones. **See the image below!**

ASHANTI PRIEST CROSSING PRAH RIVER IN NIGERIA, LONDON TIMES, 1848

The breastplate and bonnet can be found in the law of Moses, See Exodus 28:1-21 concerning the breastplate, two onyx stones and the names of the 12 tribes of Israel. What does this tell me? This tells me that the white Europeans have known since 1848 that the so-called Negro is the Jew of the Bible.

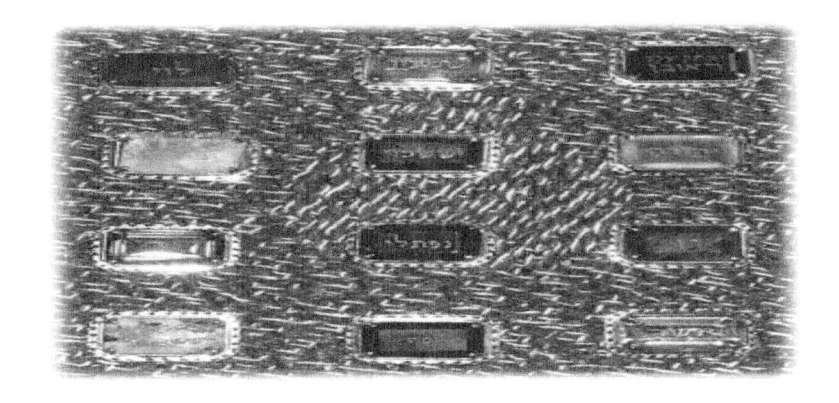

The breastplate and bonnet can be found in the law of Moses. See **Exodus 28:1, 2, 4, 9, 10, 11, 12, 17, 18, 19, 20, 21** the **breastplate**, two onyx stones and the names of the **12 tribes of Israel**. This is indisputable evidence of a great cover up; the Europeans knew who the Negro was in the Americas as early as 1800 A.D and have deliberately hidden this great truth. This would also mean the Ashanti priest had knowledge of the scriptures before they came to the shores of the Americas! What happened to the Ashanti? The Anglo-Ashanti wars were four conflicts between **the Ashanti Empire**, the Akan interior of what are now Ghana and **the British Empire** in the 19th century between 1824 and 1901. The first Anglo- Ashanti War between the two empires **(the key words are Black Ashanti Empire)** was from 1823 to 1831 where Sir Charles McCarthy and Ensign Wetherall were defeated and killed by the Ashanti and their heads were kept as trophies. In 1832 the Pra River was accepted as the border in a treaty and there were thirty years of peace. The second Anglo-Ashanti war was from 1863 to 1864, a large delegation of Ashanti crossed the Pra River seeking a fugitive. The British refused to relinquish the person and there was fighting with casualties on both sides. The 3rd Anglo-Ashanti war lasted from 1873 to 1874. In 1874 the British purchased the Dutch Gold Coast from the Dutch including Elmina which was claimed by the Ashanti. The Ashanti invaded the new British protectorate. The war was covered by Henry Morton Stanley and G.A Henty. This time the Ashanti lost and by the time the Ashanti fourth war it was all but over for the Ashanti Empire. Yaa Asante is the queen mother of the Ashanti; she was the one to lead the 4th war against the British. Ashante Prempeh shown below was a feared Ashanti king.

QUEEN YAA-ASHANTEWAA MUSEUM-GHANA   KING PREMPEH 1-ASHANTEWAA MUSEUM-GHANA

King Prempeh 1 was the 13th black Ashanti King and he also fought wars against the British Empire of whom it was said," the sun never sets on the British Empire." This saying came about because the Empire was so vast. I placed images of this black King and Queen so that your children and my children might know that the blacks in the Americas are descended from Kings. The black man can trace his lineage back to Royalty but the current Kings and Queens of Europe cannot. The current Kings of Europe have assumed the identity and titles of the black Kings who came before them! Notice the name of the queen of the Ashanti; she was named after the God of Israel...YAA or as the book of Psalms spelled it JAH, see Psalm 68:4. Make no mistake about it our fathers on the other side of the Atlantic worshipped YHWH. Later in this book we will show you how the Angle Saxon Jute gave the Negro his gods, his diet and his holydays! As you can see from the map below that the Ashanti were sold **(GOLD COAST)** as captives first in South America, and then in North America. How do I know? It has been recorded that the Ashanti or Korromante were so rebellious that the Spanish and French would not permit them into their colonies and that there was only one market open to them and that market was the British colonies. This means that the people of Ashan; the tribes of **Simeon, Judah, Benjamin and Levi** are in the Americas, Caribbean and right here in the **United States of America**. Think about this hard and long, if I can see this and I didn't major in any form of history in college (my major was Accounting), why can't the professors of the prestigious universities in America see this? How come your Pastors be they white, yellow, brown or black can't see this? Did they not go to Seminary College? Oh I forgot the Seminary colleges teach the doctrine of Rome. **Jesus said",** when the Holy Ghost comes he will lead you teach you and guide you". See the map of the North Atlantic slave trade on the next page.

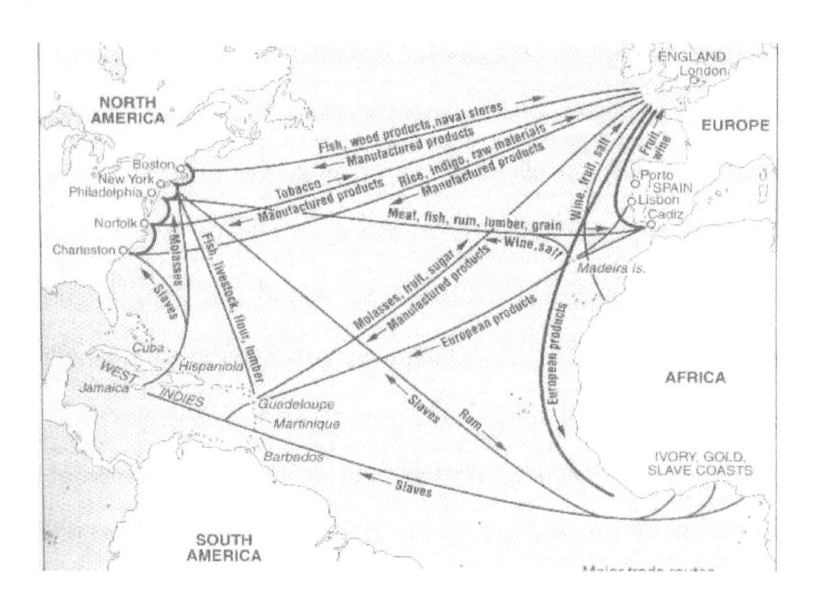

ROUTE OF THE NORTH ATLANTIC SLAVE TRADE-GOOGLE MAP

I am using this map as a visual aid to show you the routes the ships leaving Europe had to take on their voyage to West Africa. The Ashante Levites and the black Jews from the Kingdom of Judah were herded onto the same ships and brought through the Southern gate as captives.

ASHANTE/LEVITE TAKEN FROM WEST AFRICA
DEPORTED AS CAPTIVES TO;
BARBADOS
BAHAMMAS
JAMAICA
CUBA
INDIES
GUADALUPE
HISPANOLA
AMERICAS
UNITED STATES OF AMERICA

I have placed a spreadsheet in the Negro Question Part 2, the African slave ships that came from Judah. This book gives heavily researched information concerning the Countries and States that the black Jews were scattered to. I almost forgot to mention that we have in our possession a letter that was written by the Ashanti Queen to the Queen of England in which she states," the Ashanti serve the great God Nyankapon on whom men lean and do not fall, whose day of worship is Saturday and whom the Ashanti serve. See the book; Hebrewisms of West Africa, page 54, author Joseph J. Williams. If you are a true student of history you will remember that the ancient Druids were the priest of the ancient Celts. The Druid priests taught the Celts the worship of the sun god Baal. This is where the Protestant Churches and the Catholic Church get their Sunday worship from....these are ancient things.

The thing that you should take note of is this...the Ashanti were worshipping the God of Israel; keeping the Sabbath day and the feast days long before the missionaries and man stealers arrived on the Continent of Africa. Have you ever given this some thought? If the so-called Negro in the South couldn't read or write, who was it that taught him his version of Christianity? Who taught him the customs of Christmas, Easter and Halloween? It was the Roman Catholic Church! You are probably thinking to yourself why have I omitted the brothers in the North from this conversation? **The reason is simple...the brothers in the North could read, write and owned businesses....**you can find the research on this subject in the Negro Question part 6, the 13 Black Colonies....a must have book!

The school system does not teach our children how to reason or to think. **People don't understand that the British did not own the Southern States until the Louisiana Purchase of 1803.** When the 13 colonies made the Louisiana Purchase the institution of slavery came along with the land....think! England did not recognize the institution of slavery ....Prior to the Louisiana Purchase of 1803 the slave states belonged to the French. The Paris Peace treaty signed by King George proves this point perfectly.

LIBRARY OF CONGRESS PARIS PEACE TREATY 1783

"Britain acknowledges the United States <u>**New Hampshire, Massachusetts Bay, Rhode Island and Providence Plantations, Connecticut, New York, New Jersey, Pennsylvania, Delaware, Maryland, Virginia, North Carolina, South Carolina and Georgia**</u> to be free, sovereign, and independent states, and that the British Crown and all heirs and successors relinquish claims to the Government, property, and territorial rights of the same, and every part thereof." Signed by King George the 3RD.

Did you see that? There is not one mention of the Southern slave States; Mississippi, Louisiana, Arkansas, Alabama and so forth and do you know why? Britain did not own them at the time...if she did she would not made the Louisiana land purchase.

There were over one million free Negros in the North and they had been there since the colonization of North America by the black Scots under King James....the Stewart King! **I write extensively about this subject in the Negro Question Part 6, the 13 Black Colonies and the Negro Question Part 7, The Swarthy Memoirs.** It is time that we will turn our attention to the Igbo Jews of Nigeria. The Igbo are said to have migrated from Syria and Libya into West Africa. Historical records show this migration started around 640 A.D when the Arabs under the Caliphs attacked Syria. **The tribes that migrated were Dan, Naphtali, Gad, and Asher which resettled in Nigeria and became known** as the Sambatyon Jews. **In the years** 1484 and 1667 Judeans and Zebulonians from Portugal and Libya joined Sambatyon Jews of Nigeria **Jews. This was taken from the work of Chine du Nwabunwanne of Aguleri, a professor at the University of UCLA. This would also mean that the brothers had knowledge of who they were as early as 1484!**

What are the implications of such history? We know that the Nigerians were sold into this captivity because of the one word Negros despise the most, NIG*R. This word can be found on any map of Africa as NIGER, a word that denotes the location on the Gold Coast where Negros was kidnapped from. This means that the tribes of Dan, Naphtali, Gad, Judah, Benjamin and Zebulon are in the Americas', along with the tribe of Levi, the Ashanti. This has brought to pass that old prophecy in the book of Genesis 49:10, "the scepter shall not depart from Judah, or the lawgiver (Levi) from between his feet. Judah and Levi are together here in the Americas! Here is a picture of these Sambatyan Jews of Nigeria. These guys look like guys you see everyday walking in the hood. They look like brothers from the ghettos in Chicago, New York, Philadelphia, Los Angeles, and Pittsburgh, Washington. Our minds have been seared with a hot iron, **what does that mean?** The Bible says," This is a people that hate knowledge"...I suspect that this is the reason that **the Most High robbed us of our memory** of self...because we hate knowledge. You can see it in the hood today...try to teach a brother or sister knowledge and they despise it....but kick foolishness and they love you...think about it! The brothers in the Americas have spoken....they say that the brothers in America act like they are the only black Jews that were scattered out of West Africa and they are correct. The Negro Question book-series recognizes the blacks of the Americas and Caribbean as legitimate Hebrew Israelites. I heard you!

SAMBATYAN JEWS OF NIGERIA
ACADEMIC DICTIONARIES AND ENCYCLOPEDIAS

These Nigerian Jews gained official status in 1995-1997 when Israeli Prime Minister Yitzhak Rabin sent a team to Nigeria in search of the Ten Lost Tribes of Israel. **The ten tribes were spiritually lost....not physically! The ten tribes were taken captive to Assyria which is modern day Iraq and from there she went down into Africa.** This statement reeks of stupidity and I'll explain why, it is common knowledge among those in the know that on January 4, 1985 there was a secret airlift of Ethiopian Jews into the land of Israel.

**ETHIOPIAN JEWS BEING AIRLIFTED TO ISRAEL
GOOGLE-AIR LIFT OF ETHIOPIAN JEWS**

Operation Solomon took place in 1991 bringing 14,000 Ethiopian Jews to Israel, culminating with the arrival of about 40,000 Ethiopian Jews. The scene with the Ethiopian Jews being airlifted to Israel reminds me of the scripture concerning the gathering of Israel. See **Isaiah 60:8, who are these that fly as a cloud, and as the doves to their windows?** This isn't ancient history, you don't have to dig in the ground to find this information; this is practically a current event! Didn't the Lord have the prophet Amos to write, Amos 9:7, **art not you as the children of Ethiopia unto me?** And in another place, Jeremiah 13:23 can the Ethiopian change his skin or a leopard his spots?

BETA ISRAEL OF ETHIOPIA-GOOGLE BETA ISRAEL

The Beta Israel cite the 9th century testimony of Eldad ha dani (the Danite), from a time before even the Zagwean dynasty was established. Eldad was a Jewish man of dark skin who suddenly turned up in Egypt and created a great stir in the Egyptian Jewish community and elsewhere in the Mediterranean Jewish communities he travelled to. He claimed that he had come from a Jewish kingdom of pastoralists far to the south. The only language he spoke was a hitherto unknown dialect of Hebrew. Although he strictly followed the Mosaic commandments his observance differed in some details from rabbinic halakhah, so that some thought he might be a Karaite, even if his practice differed from theirs too. He carried Hebrew books with him that supported his explanations of halakhah, and he was able to cite ancient authorities in the sagely traditions of his own people. He said that the Jews of his own kingdom derived from the tribe of Dan, which had fled the civil war in the Kingdom of Israel between Solomon's son Rehoboam and Jeroboam the son of Nebat, by resettling in Egypt. From there they moved southwards up the Nile into Ethiopia, and the Beta Israel say this confirms that they are descended from the tribe of Dan. Some Beta Israel however, assert even nowadays that their Danite origins go back to the time of Moses himself, when some Danites parted from other Jews right after the Exodus and moved south to Ethiopia. Eldad the Danite does indeed speak of at least three waves of Jewish immigration into his region, creating other Jewish tribes and kingdoms, including the earliest wave that settled in a remote kingdom of the tribe of Moses. This was the strongest and most secure Jewish kingdom of all, with farming villages, cities and great wealth. The Mosaic claims of the Beta Israel, in any case, like those of the Zagwe dynasty itself, are clearly very ancient. Sources tell of many Jews who were brought as prisoners of war from ancient Israel by Ptolemy I and also settled on the border of his kingdom with Nubia (Sudan). Another tradition handed down in the community from father to son asserts that they arrived either via the old district of Qwara in northwestern Ethiopia, or via the Atbara River, where the Nile tributaries flow into Sudan. Some accounts even specify the route taken by their forefathers on their way upstream from Egypt. The Beta Israelites lived in north and northwestern Ethiopia. Nearly 120,000 of these black Ethiopian Jews have been allowed to return to Israel under **operation Moses 1984, operation Sheba 1985** and of course the aforementioned **operation Solomon 1991**. The white Jews in Israel are flawed in that they think they have a monopoly on who is Israel and who isn't. The Lord told Moses that Israel would be scattered into every nation under the sun and Africa has today 54 nations. A bit of world history demands a place in this book. There was a secret meeting among the European colonizing nations in Europe called the Belgium conference presided over by King Leopold of Belgium **(known as the butcher)** in the year 1884. This meeting that was held was to decide the fate of 53 African nations. Of great interest is that none of the African nations were invited. The reason for the snub was that the Europeans had decided to carve Africa up among themselves to steal the raw materials and goods and this began the period of Globalization oops my bad, I meant colonization! The only nation not to be colonized was Ethiopia. You see Napoleon Bonaparte had bankrupted Europe with the Napoleonic wars and these Europeans were in an economic recession and they figured let's make Africa pay for it and so they did. The only nation that wasn't colonized was Ethiopia with thanks in large part to King Haile Selassie. Ethiopia had to remain black, because it was written in Amos 9:7 Art not thou as the Ethiopian unto me and Jeremiah 13:23 can the Ethiopian change his spots? The Greeks called the Ethiopians burnt face, this is how black he was and he had to remain black for a generation to come, and that generation is us (2019). For the sake of our young people, I put a picture of an authentic black king **(Haile Selassie)** who the Europeans and the naysayers cannot deny that he lived and that he was black! This will prove to our children that we once were kings and that our current state of affairs is not indicative of who we are!

**KING HAILE SELASSIE OF ETHIOPIA, 1930-1974
NATIONAL MUSEUM OF ETHIOPIA**

King Haile Selassie 1 traces his lineage back to Solomon the son of David. King Selassie went before the League of Nations **(the European colonizing nations)** to plead the cause of his people after Benito Mussolini and the Italian people invaded Ethiopia using chemical warfare. His speech at the League of Nations has been regarded as one of the greatest speeches in the 20th century. This is an interesting fact, did you know that the **colonizing European nation members that appeared at the Belgium conference in 1888** were the **same good old boy European nations who started the League of Nations in 1927** and who were the **same good old boy nations who started the United Nations in 1948?** Guess who was not invited to sit down at the round table (membership) on all three occasions? Yes, 53 African nations, the United Nations didn't include Africa until the African Nationalists on the continent cleaned out all of the European thieves in 1960. They did a noble job of kicking the Globalists out of their countries and then committed a foolish act; they took loans with interest rates that they have not been able to pay back. If the International Monetary Fund and the World Bank were righteous organizations.....they would forgive the debt.

THE NRI TRIBE OF NIGERIA

The NRI KINGDOM is the oldest Kingdom in Nigeria. It was founded around 900AD by the progenitor, Eri, the son of Gad. According to biblical accounts, Jacob had Leah as his wife who begot four sons for him. When Leah noticed she had passed child-bearing age, she gave her maid - servant, Zilpah to Jacob to wife, and through Zilpah he had a son named Gad. **Gad then bigot Eri,** who later formed a clan known as **Erites; see Genesis Chapter 30 verse 9, Genesis chapter 46 verse 16 and Numbers chapter 26 verses 15-19.** Upon closer inspection of the tribe, a temple was discovered **with the inscription holy to Gad** and an onyx stone with **Gads name written in ancient Hebrew.**

IMAGE LOCATION-AGULERI NIGERIA- ERI THE SON OF GAD

The Igbo's are said to have descended from the tribe of Zevulun ben-Ya`aqov, who was the 5th son of Ya`aqov (Jacob). This lineage comprises of the UbuluOkiti, UbuluUkwu, in Delta State, who settled in Ubululhejiofor. According to tradition, it is said that a descendent of the tribe of Zevulun (ZEBULUN) named Zevulunu, on the advice of a certain Levite, married a woman from Oji, whom descended from the tribe of Judah, and from this union was born Ozubulu **ben-Zebulunu**. It is said that Ozubulu then went on to have 4 sons of his own who settled into other parts of the region. These sons being: Amakwa, from whom a clan in Neni, anambra state descended and Egbema, from whom the EgbemaUgwuta clan in Imo State and the OhajiEgbema clan in Rivers state descended **Benei Menash**: of whom descended the tribe of Manasah. **Could this be the reason that the original homeland that the Europeans had sought for the white Jews was Africa (ancient Libya) before they settled on Palestine?** Beni Zebulon and Beni Menash is an ancient Hebrew phrase that means, born of! This phraseology can be found in ancient Paleo Hebrew manuscripts (Moabite Stele) that was found in ancient Anatolia.

This artifact reads," I'm King Masha' <u>Bana King Masha</u> King of Moab. The wording is identical to beni Zebulu and beni Menash. Beni means bana of or born of just like in the Moabite stele. I find it hard to believe the so-called scholars missed this!

Ben Yoseph, who was one of the grandsons of Ya`aqov (Jacob) through his 11th son Yoseph (Joseph). According to the Torah Jacob claimed both Manasseh and his brother Ephraim as his own sons. It is theorized by some that this is the possible lineage of the Amichi, Ichi, Nnewi-Ichi clans. Here is a map below showing the location of Nigeria, you should notice that east of Nigeria is the Bight of Benin (Bight- a bay that 400 miles long) it has been estimated that over one million Igbo's were transported

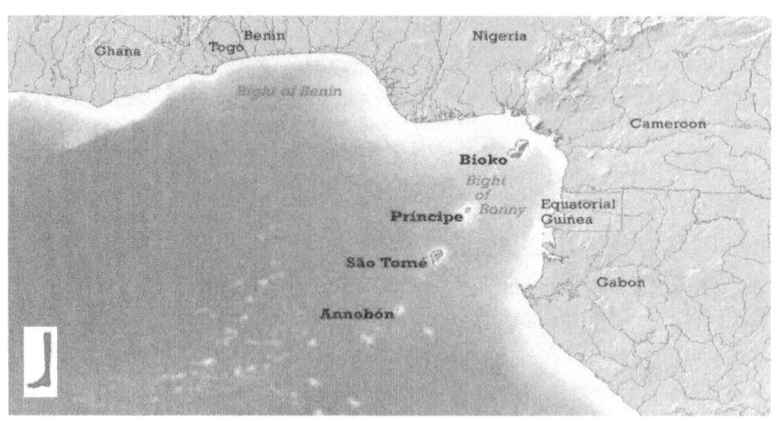

BIGHT OF BENIN-GOOGLE MAPS

from this area to Virginia, Kentucky, and Maryland. It is said that 60% of all African Americans have at least one Igbo ancestor! The word Okra is an Igbo word. I don't know who you are but if you are old school you have definitely eaten Okra in your lifetime and if not you....surely big mama, your great aunts and uncles ate okra. I have eaten Okra and still do from time to time.....its okay.

IGBOS JEWS OF WEST AFRICA
THE DISPERSION OF ZEBULUN-MANASSAH AND EPHRAIM

> JAMAICA
> CUBA
> HAITI
> BARBADOS
> BELIZE
> TRINIDAD
> TOBAGO
> MARYLAND
> VIRGINIA
> GEORGIA

Why am I so convinced that these brothers from Nigeria are the tribes of **Manasseh, Ephraim and Benjamin?** The way the scribe wrote his family history is ancient and can be dated as far back as 840 B.C. Consider the sentence structure below.

"The Igbo's are said to have descended from the tribe of Zevulun ben-Ya`aqov."

This is exactly how the wording on the Moabite Stele is constructed and the Igbo's use the same structure; ben of Yaaqov or born of Jacob. **The Igbos also spell the name of Jacob correctly in ancient Hebrew minus the letter V. The translator of the King James New Testament uses similar structure.** In the book of Luke (Luke 3:23 & 24) it reads, and Jesus himself ...the son of Joseph, which was the son of Heli; Verse 24 which was the son of Mathat. This is what the Gentiles call scholarship!

LEMBA TRIBE OF SOUTH AFRICA

IMAGE OF LEMBA MEN AT SABBATH SERVICE
GETTY IMAGES

Tudor Parfitt a protagonist of the **NOVA DOCUMENTARY**, The Lost Tribes of Israel, made a trip to South Africa to study the Lemba tribe and their traditions. He wrote that he observed their customs of keeping the Sabbath, not eating blood in their food, their keeping of the dietary law, and circumcising of their sons on the 8th day. Based on these observations Mr. Parfitt came to the conclusion that the Lemba people's customs were Semitic and not Hamitic (African). I liked this guys work to the max but he failed to mention one thing and that is that the Lemba history. The Lemba have been keeping the Law of circumcision and other Hebraic customs for thousands of years. In fact when the white missionaries came to Africa they already knew about Jesus. In order to prove or disprove the assertions of the Lemba tribe he undertook a venture with the Center for Genetic Anthropology in London, they identified a Y chromosome marker on Lemba males and compared that to Bantu Africans, Yemini Arabs, Sephardic Jews, Ashkenazi Jews and the Cohanim. NOVA team Dr. David Goldstein commented the Lemba Y (Bubba clan) chromosome was a match with the Cohen chromosome identified in the Jewish priesthood! Also of particular interest is the fact that they sought out **Bantu Africans**. Let's deviate for a moment, as you might have not known there are about **250 Bantu place names in South Carolina. Bantu speaking people were found in Angola, Rwanda, Burundi, Zimbabwe and South Africa**. The Bantu speaking people of Angola were first brought to Brazil by the Portuguese. There was research done by **Dr. Joseph P Holloway** a professor at California State University at Northridge which provides extremely useful information. He found Bantu place names in Alabama, Georgia, Florida, Mississippi, North Carolina, South Carolina and Virginia. What does this mean? **It's quite simple, it proves that black Jews associated with the Lemba tribe (Bantu speaking people) were held captive in the south and that upon the great migration of Negros from 1910 to 1930 and the years 1940 to 1970 these black Jews saturated the northern cities** of America.

REPLICA ARK OF THE COVENANT
ZIMBABWE AFRICA-700 YEARS OLD

This reminded me of when the children of Israel were parceling out the land of Canaan in the book of Joshua 22: 9-34. The tribes on the other side of Jordan built an altar to the Lord and this was their logic; the tribe of Ruben, Gad and the half tribe of Manasseh stated that the reason they built the facsimile altar was so that the other tribes could not boast one day that they were not Israelites. This image of the replica Ark of the Covenant that was found in South Africa reeks of the same reasoning; it appears that our fathers left relics behind to remind us of who we really are!

CHAPTER 4   THE SHIPS OF BABEL

IMAGE LOCATION PINTEREST-CREATOR UNKNOWN

I named this chapter the ships of Babel, because Babel means confusion and when the kidnappers of black human flesh brought in the blacks of Africa they were confused into thinking that since everybody was black that they were all African. In Genesis (Genesis 11: 9) Verse 9, **therefore is the name of it called Babel because the Lord did there confound** the language of all the earth and from thence did the Lord scatter them abroad upon the face of all the earth. In Deuteronomy28:68 the Lord said he would bring Israel back into Egypt on ships and this is exactly what happened to the Negro, he came into captivity on ships. **Notice all of these blacks, some Egyptians, some Canaanites, some Elamites, some Hebrews, and some Arabs, in the same ship. Can you tell the African (Ham) from the Hebrew (Shem)?**

If nothing else this should alert you to this great problem in the black community. We have been mixed together like mixed vegetables ...we look alike but are genetically different. Is there a solution to this problem? Yes...not to worry the Lord has a record of everyone on this Earth. In the book of Psalm (Psalm 87:5 & 6) verse 6 **the Lord shall count when he writes up the people that this man was born here.** See Luke 12:7, **the very hairs of your head are numbered**...so don't worry God is in control!

The point that I am trying to make is that the European kidnapper couldn't make the distinction between the black African (son of Ham) and the black Mesopotamian (black Hebrew Israelite). On the next page I have a special treat for you, it is a $100 dollar confederate bill depicting the so called Negro hoeing and picking cotton. I bet you didn't know that the Negro was once on the face of American money did you? **See the next page.**

1861 CONFEDERATE $100 BILL SHOWING NEGRO CAPTIVES PICKING COTTON

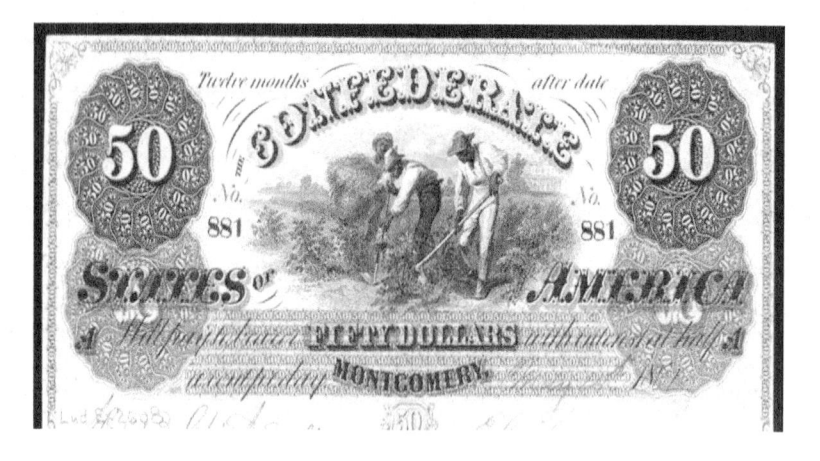

NATIONAL MUSEUM OF AMERICAN HISTORY

The white establishment can never say they didn't make merchandise of the Negro because he put the Negro on his confederate money as a propaganda tool. These blacks are reaping cotton in Montgomery Alabama....and yet....they don't want to pay the so-called Negro reparations....they paid the European Jews and they paid the Japanese Americans ...why not us?

The black captive was brought to America via the southern gate (the south) but remember there was a great migration of Negros from the South to the North from 1910 to 1930. Plus another migration took place from 1940 to 1970 relocating over 5 million Negros from the brutality of the south. It is quite simple and apparent that the black Jews of Africa are right here in the United States of America, Caribbean and the Americas. There is a curse and prophecy written in the book of Deuteronomy the 32nd chapter and the 68th verse which states," Israel would go back into Egypt on ships as bond men and bond women and that Israel would not see the land again."**There is no other nation on earth that went into bondage on ships but us**. It happened in A.D 70 when we were carted off to Rome under Vespasian Caesar and his son Titus Caesar. See Deuteronomy 28:46 and these (curses) shall be on upon thee for a sign and for a wonder and upon thy seed forever! Why did the Lord use the verbiage on you for a sign? Because a sign can talk, the Lord knew that when the Negro got out of his hard bondage he wouldn't know how to read or write…the slavers made sure of this in the South. **The free blacks in the North could read, write and they owned businesses.** Reading and writing separates humanity from the beast Kingdom. You will never be able to form your own nation if you can't keep records because when a generation dies you will have to continue starting over….. **READ!!!**

The so-called Negro was supposed to see himself in the various signs that God had the prophets to write in the scriptures! The Negro was supposed to be quickened by the signs but **there are other forces at work keeping him in darkness; Television, radio, sports, newspapers, concerts, parties, drinking, getting high, selling drugs, gang banging, all of these things are keeping 42 million Negros in America from waking up!** There was a time during slavery that the Negro would risk his life and limb to learn how to read but now he has been reduced to a Willie Lynch state. This is the condition of the entire earth right now. Case in point, when the uprisings occurred in Egypt the Mubarak regime cut off the internet, texting and cell phones. This happened in Egypt, Libya, and Bahrain. This is the ideology **(Thinking)** of the power structure in this world. **The Bible said," the people perish for lack of knowledge",** and this has become very evident with the actions of the nations. Right here in America our government is trying to place the internet under the security act. That means that they will have the power in times of national interest to shut it down! Through the World Wide Web the Earth has become one big neighborhood, what happens in one nation overnight is heard around the world the same night! The Chinese are no different than the Arab nations who have suppressed the 1% with the shutting down of social media. In China the people are in darkness, they have a 2010 Nobel Peace Prize winner by the name of Liu Xiaobo but he has been censored, meaning the people of China don't even know he won the award! Via the internet we have access to all the libraries and history of the world uncensored by the ruling governments of the world. The powers that be are afraid of you obtaining knowledge because as your knowledge increases the vail of darkness falls off of your eyes and you can see. All over Arabia, in nations revolting the regimes are cutting off the internet, text messaging and tweeting. Open your eyes and see.... if the method to control and deceive 42 million Negros can work over a 392 year period , why not do it to the whole world? This is how the elite maintain control over the masses, truly knowledge is power. The mindset is if you can keep the Negro in darkness he will be our servants forever, this was the mindset among the Southern white slave owners. This is the condition that the Negro community finds itself in today in America, educated in the educational institutions of the west, but educated in what? The grammar schools, high schools, and colleges in the United States have been set up for one thing, to teach entire generations lies and to indoctrinate them into the history about European nations and white people, **this is the first law of darkness**. Hide a man's truth about himself, from himself and then teach him the history of the **(European)** oppressor every time he shows up for schooling. Teach him to hate everything about himself and anybody that looks like him!

JACOBITES ARRIVE ON THE SHORES OF AMERICA 1619
COLONISTS OR SLAVES?

IMAGES FROM THE TOMB OF BENI HASAN IN EGYPT

TABLET READS-THE PEOPLE OF AMO OR AM'

These images were taken from the tomb of Beni Hassan in Egypt. These are images of the ancient black Hebrew Israelites going into Egypt, notice the men, women and children are black;

the men have afros and beards. On the second row of pictures the last one to the right the black Hebrew is holding out a tablet that reads the people of Amo". Once the tablet was interpreted it reads, "The people of God! In the book of Isaiah, the 49th chapter verse 15 reads, can a woman forget her sucking child, that she should not have compassion on the son of her womb: yeah, **they may forget yet will I not forget thee.** Verse 16 behold I have graven thee upon the palms of my hands; thy walls are continually before me. The God of Israel hid all of this information concerning the true people of Israel in tombs and pyramids from those who destroyed the pictures of the prophets and the apostles. Think for a moment when Jesus took Peter, James and John with him up into the mount where he was transfigured before them it was written that the apostles recognized Moses and Elijah. This would imply that they had seen pictures of the elders because Moses and Elijah lived almost 2000 years before the apostles had ever been born! We now have images of Abraham, Moses, Aaron, Sarah, the prophet Isaiah, King David and Solomon. The History channel did a special on the pyramids of Egypt and stumbled on this truth but it wasn't emphasized during the special. The sight of these images and the interpretation of the writing tablet blew me away but notice something else. The truth has been locked up behind bars! These are the people that came into the North Atlantic Slave Trade **the Ammo or the people of AM'**, who have been bitterly mistreated by the Europeans. Once our fathers arrived here in America we were sold as chattel **(same word cattle)**.See Deuteronomy 28: 49, 50, 68 you need to read the entire chapter to get some understanding. The Lord had it written that the nation that would take us back into captivity would have the eagle as its standard (America) and that Israel would be sold as bondmen and bondwomen.

The historians in North America teach that slaves came into Virginia in the year 1619 and yet this is not accurate. It is impossible that Virginia was a slave State in 1619 because King James was still alive and at that time.....England did not believe in the institution of slavery! Read the English Magna Carta. King James Stewart was King James the 6th of Scotland who became King James the 1st of England....fact. Keep reading and you will see.

That is why I was extremely amused by the propaganda of the 70's and 80's where it was said that black women didn't need a black man. **If you are a black woman reading this book remember this, you are still a part of the Negro struggle whether you believe it or not.** The fate of the black woman and child is woven together with the fate of the black man! When you get some time black woman and black man... read the book of Esther the 3rd and 4th chapter. In the 4th chapter of Esther, the 13th and 14th verse, Mordecai put it very bluntly to Esther and told her "don't think you will escape because of your position in the kingdom." I am saying the same thing to you sisters and brothers in the corporate sector: Don't fool yourself, you have been included in the Negro Census (42 million), no matter what your status is in America....**you are still part of the Negro question!** How was the European able to keep a strong people like the Negro in captivity? 1818: A letter from "Judex" (a court arbitrator) in Leesburg's *Genius of Liberty*, warns **that teaching slaves to read and write is illegal**. **"Negroes, teachers and justices look to it: the order of society must prevail over the notions of individuals."** The sons of the Empire were not simply imprisoned in America, the Negro was placed in complete darkness, the kind of darkness you see when you enter his penal system, the darkness of the mind! **If you have black teen aged children** in your home or in your family, please get them this book; it will begin to answer a lot of questions in their minds concerning the condition that he finds himself in America.

The first law of Darkness has been amended by the elite, the amendment to the law; it is okay in this generation for the Negro to learn how to read and write as long as he is reading information that we provide for him (indoctrination). This means we can still control him without the physical chains of bondage. You see the new chains will be the chaining of his mind, feed him," **a version of European history**," teach him nothing about himself, take the Negro champions of history and make them white so the Negro will think he had never accomplished anything. Haven't you notice that every time black history month comes around they start it off with the slave trade and commence it with the civil rights movement? They are subconsciously keeping the Negro in a slave like mentality via their propaganda tool.... Hollywood. **The narrative concerning the black slaves entering Virginia in 1619 has changed. The new research suggests that the 13 British colonies were founded by the black Scottish, Germans and black Irish.** The research that proves this truth is in this book but you must continue to read; you will see medieval artifacts, ships manifests, eye witness accounts and research from noted European geneticists which shall validate my claims.

CHAPTER 5   THE NEGRO RESISTANCE

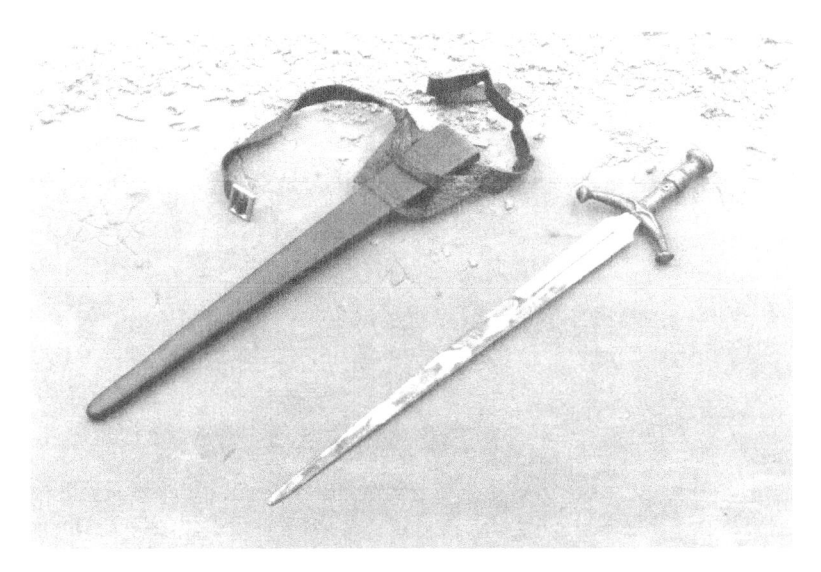

GOOGLE BLOODY SWORD

If you read the narrative (story) concerning the North Atlantic Slave trade you will leave thinking that the black man was weak and a coward....on the contrary. **This chapter will deal with the fight that the black man put up against an adversary that had the advantage in reading, writing, and the sell out Negro!** I must warn you of all the odds that the black man has fought against in America....**the sell out Negro is the most formidable** because by the time you realize he is in the midst.....it is too late! **The sell out Negro** cares not for his people...his only aim in life is how he can accumulate material wealth at the expense of his own people!

**TOUSSAINT L OVERTURE, 1743-1803
HAITI MUSEUM**

Toussaint L. Overture was a captive in Haiti and led a revolt defeating a sizeable British, Spanish and American force of about 10,000 men. Toussaint became Governor for life and freed the slaves of San Domingo….this was the first French slave Dominion to fall during the institution of slavery. The thing that the slavers feared the most had come upon them….a black insurrection! L Overture Toussaint made one critical mistake…he accepted a meeting with Napoleon Bonaparte to make peace between France and Haiti. **The acceptance of peace was not the problem,** his problem was that he boarded a ship and went to France….**big mistake!** Once Toussaint arrived in France he was imprisoned in a dungeon until the day of his death in 1803.

HAITI SOLDIERS FOUGHT IN THE AMERICAN REVOLUTION

One of the greatest secrets concerning the American Revolution, **there are many,** four thousand free black Haitian Frenchmen fought on the side of the American colonists in its revolt against the Crown of England; the system places the number at 500 men. This all black Haitian unit fought in the battle of Savannah Georgia, Charleston Sc 1780, Pensacola Fl, Sarasota Fl 1781 and in Yorktown in 1781. In 2007 the city of Savannah Georgia **erected a monument concerning the Haitian sacrifice and this untaught truth.** Trusting the Government sponsored School system to teach your children the truth is like jumping in a lion cage dripping in blood and hoping the lion doesn't eat you….real talk!

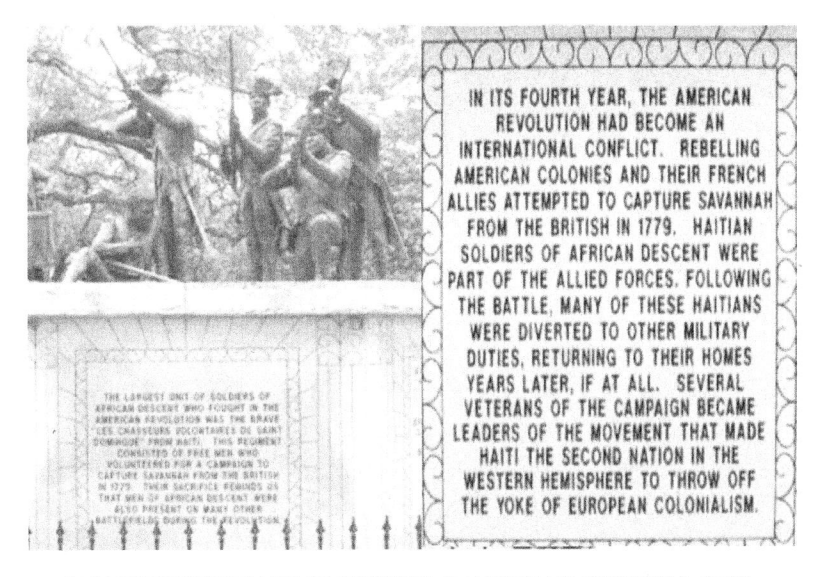

IN ITS FOURTH YEAR, THE AMERICAN REVOLUTION HAD BECOME AN INTERNATIONAL CONFLICT. REBELLING AMERICAN COLONIES AND THEIR FRENCH ALLIES ATTEMPTED TO CAPTURE SAVANNAH FROM THE BRITISH IN 1779. HAITIAN SOLDIERS OF AFRICAN DESCENT WERE PART OF THE ALLIED FORCES. FOLLOWING THE BATTLE, MANY OF THESE HAITIANS WERE DIVERTED TO OTHER MILITARY DUTIES, RETURNING TO THEIR HOMES YEARS LATER, IF AT ALL. SEVERAL VETERANS OF THE CAMPAIGN BECAME LEADERS OF THE MOVEMENT THAT MADE HAITI THE SECOND NATION IN THE WESTERN HEMISPHERE TO THROW OFF THE YOKE OF EUROPEAN COLONIALISM.

MONUMENT FRANKLIN STREET, SAVANNAH GEORGIA-2007

NAT TURNER- WOOD CUTTING-NATIONAL ARCHIVE   **THOMAS R. GRAY BIOGRAPHIES**

I was always taught that there is a time for everything under the sun; a time to live and a time to die, a time to speak and a time to be silent. It is time for me to be silent and let Nat Turner tell his own story….. in his own words…let's listen! **See the next page.**

THE CONFESSIONS OF NAT TURNER

LIBRARY OF CONGRESS SUBJECT HEADING S 21ST EDITION

DISTRICT OF COLUMBIA, TO WIT:

Be it remembered, That on this tenth day of November, Anno Domini, eighteen hundred and thirty-one, Thomas R. Gray of the said District, deposited in this office the title of a book, which is in the words as following:

"The Confessions of Nat Turner, the leader of the late insurrection in Southampton, Virginia, as fully and voluntarily made to Thomas R. Gray, in the prison where he was confined, and acknowledged by him to be such when read before the Court of Southampton; with the certificate, under seal, of the Court convened at Jerusalem, November 5, 1831, for his trial. **Also, an authentic account of the whole insurrection, with lists of the whites who were murdered, and of the negroes brought before the Court of Southampton,** and there sentenced, &c. the right whereof he claims as proprietor, in conformity with an Act of Congress, entitled "An act to amend the several acts respecting Copy Rights."

NAT TURNER IN HIS OWN WORDS!

"**The great day of judgment was at Hand.** About this time I told these things to a white man, (Etheldred T. Brantley) on whom it had a wonderful effect--and he ceased from his wickedness, and was attacked immediately with a coetaneous eruption, and blood oozed from the pores of his skin, and after praying and fasting nine days, he was healed, and the Spirit appeared to me again, and said, as the Savoir had been baptized so should we be also--and **when the white people would not let us be baptized by the church, we went down into the water together, in the sight of many who reviled us, and were baptized by the Spirit--**After this I rejoiced greatly, and gave thanks to God. And on the 12th of May, 1828, I heard a loud noise in the heavens, and the Spirit instantly appeared to me and said the Serpent was loosened, and Christ had laid down the yoke he had borne for the sins of men, and that I should take it on and fight against the

Serpent, for the time was fast approaching when the first should be last and the last should be first. *Ques.* Do you not find yourself mistaken now? *Ans.* Was not Christ crucified. And **by signs in the heavens that it would make known to me when I should commence the great work--and until the first sign appeared, I should conceal it from the knowledge of men--And on the appearance of the sign, (the eclipse of the sun last February) I should arise and prepare myself, and slay my enemies with their own weapons.** And immediately on the sign appearing in the heavens, the seal was removed from my lips, and I communicated the great work laid out for me to do, to four in whom I had the greatest confidence, (Henry, Hark, Nelson, and Sam)--It was intended by us to have begun the work of death on the 4th July last--Many were the plans formed and rejected by us, and it affected my mind to such a degree, that I fell sick, and the time passed without our coming to any determination how to commence--**Still forming new schemes and rejecting them, when the sign appeared again,** <u>which determined me not to wait longer.</u> Since the commencement of 1830, I had been living with Mr. Joseph Travis, who was to me a kind master, and placed the greatest confidence in me; in fact, I had no cause to complain of his treatment to me. On Saturday evening, the 20th of August, it was agreed between Henry, Hark and myself, to prepare a dinner the next day for the men we expected, and then to concert a plan, as we had not yet determined on any. Hark, on the following morning, brought a pig, and Henry brandy, and being joined by Sam, Nelson,

Page 12

Will and Jack, they prepared in the woods a dinner, where, about three o'clock, I joined them.

Q. Why were you so backward in joining them?

A. The same reason that had caused me not to mix with them for years before.

I saluted them on coming up, and asked Will how came he there, he answered, his life was worth no more than others, and his liberty as dear to him. I asked him if he thought to obtain it? He said he would, or lose his life. This was enough to put him in full confidence. Jack, I knew, was only a tool in the hands of Hark, **it was quickly agreed we should commence at home (Mr. J. Travis') on that night,** and until we had armed and equipped ourselves, and gathered sufficient force, neither age nor sex was to be spared, (which was invariably adhered to.) We remained at the feast until about two hours in the night, when we went to the house and found Austin; they all went to the cider press and drank, except myself. On returning to the house, Hark went to the door with an axe, for the purpose of breaking it open, as we knew we were strong enough to murder the family, if they were awaked by the noise; but reflecting that it might create an alarm in the neighborhood, we determined to enter the house secretly, and murder them whilst sleeping. **Hark got a ladder and set it against the chimney, on which I ascended, and hoisting a window, entered and came down stairs, unbarred the door, and removed the guns from their places. It was then observed that I must spill the first blood. On which, armed with a hatchet, and accompanied by Will, I entered my master's chamber, it being dark, I could not give a death blow, the hatchet glanced from his head, he sprang from the bed and called his wife, it was his last word, Will laid him dead, with a blow of his axe, and Mrs. Travis shared the same fate, as she lay in bed. The murder of this family, five in number, was the work of a moment, not one of them awoke; there was a little infant sleeping in a cradle, that was forgotten, until we had left the house and gone some distance, when Henry and Will returned and killed it;** we got here, four guns that would shoot, and several old muskets, with a pound or two of powder. We remained some time at the barn, where we paraded; I formed them in a line as soldiers, and after carrying them through all the maneuvers I was master of, marched them **off to Mr. Salathul Francis', about six hundred yards distant. Sam and Will went to the door and knocked. Mr. Francis asked who was there, Sam replied, it was him, and he had a letter for him, on which he got up and came to the door, they immediately seized him, and dragging him out a little from the door, he was dispatched by repeated blows on the head;** there was no other white person in the family. **We started from there for Mrs. Reese's,** maintaining the most perfect silence on our march, where finding the door unlocked, we entered, and murdered Mrs. Reese in her bed, while sleeping; her son awoke, but it was only to sleep the sleep of death, he had only time to say who is that, and he was no more. From Mrs. Reese's we went to Mrs. Turner's, a mile distant, which we reached about sunrise, on Monday morning. Henry, Austin, and Sam, went to the still, where, finding Mr. Peebles, Austin shot him, and the rest of us went to the house; as we approached, the family discovered us, and shut the door. Vain hope! Will, with one stroke of his axe, opened it, and we entered and found Mrs. Turner and Mrs. Newsome in the middle of a room, almost frightened to death. Will immediately killed Mrs. Turner, with one blow of his axe. I took Mrs. Newsome by the hand, and with the sword I had when I was apprehended, I struck her several blows over the head, but not being able to kill her, as the sword was dull. Will turning around and discovering it, dispatched her also. A general destruction of property and search for money and ammunition always succeeded the murders. By this time my company amounted to fifteen, and nine men mounted, who started for Mrs. Whitehead's, (the other six were to go through a by way to Mr. Bryant's and rejoin us at Mrs. Whitehead's,) as we approached the house we discovered Mr. Richard Whitehead standing in the cotton patch, near the lane fence; we called him over into the lane, and Will, the executioner, was near at hand, with his fatal axe, to send him to an untimely grave. As we pushed on to the house, I discovered some one run round the garden, and thinking it was some of the white family, I pursued them, but finding it was a servant girl belonging to the house, **I returned to commence the work of death, but they whom I left, had not been idle; all the family were already murdered, but Mrs. Whitehead and her daughter Margaret. As I came round to the door I saw Will pulling Mrs. Whitehead out of the house, and at the step he nearly severed her head from her body, with his broad axe. Miss Margaret, when I discovered her, had concealed herself in the corner, formed by the projection of the cellar cap from the house; on my approach she fled, but was soon overtaken, and after**

repeated blows with a sword, I killed her by a blow on the head, with a fence rail. By this time, the six who had gone by Mr. Bryant's, rejoined us, and informed me they had done the work of death assigned them. We again divided, part going to Mr. Richard Porter's, and from thence to Nathaniel Francis', the others to Mr. Howell Harris', and Mr. T. Doyles. On my reaching Mr. Porter's, he had escaped with his family. I understood there, that the alarm had already spread, and I immediately returned to bring up those sent to Mr. Doyles, and Mr. Howell Harris'; the party I left going on to Mr. Francis', having told them I would join them in that neighborhood. **I met these sent to Mr. Doyles' and Mr. Harris' returning, having met Mr. Doyle on the road and killed him**; and learning from some who joined them, that Mr. Harris was from home, I immediately pursued the course taken by the party gone on before; but knowing they would complete the work of death and pillage, at Mr. Francis' before **I could there, I went to Mr. Peter Edwards', expecting to find them there, but they had been here also. I then went to Mr. John T. Barrow's; they had been here and murdered him**. I pursued on their track to Capt. Newit Harris', where I found the greater part mounted, and ready to start; the men now amounting to about forty, shouted and hurrahed as I rode up, some were in the yard, loading their guns, others drinking. They said Captain Harris and his family had escaped, the property in the house they destroyed, robbing him of money and other valuables. I ordered them to mount and march instantly, this was about nine or ten o'clock, Monday morning. I proceeded to Mr. Levi Waller's, two or three miles distant. I took my station in the rear, and as it was my object to carry terror and devastation wherever we went, I placed fifteen or twenty of the best armed and most to be relied on, in front, who generally approached the houses as fast as their horses could run; this was for two purposes, to prevent their escape and strike terror to the inhabitants--on this account I never got to the houses, after leaving Mrs. Whitehead's, until the murders were committed, except in one case. **I sometimes got in sight in time to see the work of death completed, viewed the mangled bodies as they lay, in silent satisfaction, and immediately started in quest of other victims--Having murdered Mrs. Waller and**

ten children, we started for Mr. William Williams' --having killed him and two little boys that were there; while engaged in this, Mrs. Williams fled and got some distance

from the house, but she was pursued, overtaken, and compelled to get up behind one of the company, who brought her back, and after showing her the mangled body of her lifeless husband, she was told to get down and lay by his side, where she was shot dead. I then started for Mr. Jacob Williams, where the family was murdered--**Here we found a young man named Drury, who had come on business with Mr. Williams--he was pursued, overtaken and shot. Mrs. Vaughan was the next place we visited--and after murdering the family here, I determined on starting for Jerusalem--** Our number amounted now to fifty or sixty, all mounted and armed with guns, axes, swords and clubs-- On reaching Mr. James W. Parkers' gate, immediately on the road leading to Jerusalem, and about three miles distant, it was proposed to me to call there, but I objected, as I knew he was gone to Jerusalem, and my object was to reach there as soon as possible; but some of the men having relations at Mr. Parker's it was agreed that they might call and get his people.

THE CAPTURE OF NAT TURNER

"Pursuing our course back and coming in sight of Captain Harris', where we had been the day before, we discovered a party of white men at the house, on which all deserted me but two, (Jacob and Nat,) we concealed ourselves in the woods until near night, when I sent them in search of Henry, Sam, Nelson, and Hark, and directed them to rally all they could, at the place we had had our dinner the Sunday before, where they would find me, and I accordingly returned there as soon as it was dark and remained until Wednesday evening, **when discovering white men riding around the place as though they were looking for someone, and**

none of my men joining me, I concluded Jacob and Nat had been taken, and compelled to betray me. On this I gave up all hope for the present; and on Thursday night after having supplied myself with provisions from Mr. Travis's, I scratched a hole under a pile of fence rails in a field, where I concealed myself for six weeks, never leaving my hiding place but for a few minutes in the dead of night to get water which was very near; thinking by this time I could venture out, I began to go about in the night and eaves drop the houses in the neighborhood; pursuing this course for about a fortnight and gathering little or no intelligence, afraid of speaking to any human being, and returning every morning to my cave before the dawn of day. **I know not how long I might have led this life, if accident had not betrayed me, a dog in the neighborhood passing by my hiding place one night while I was out, was attracted by some meat I had in my cave, and crawled in and stole it, and was coming out just as I returned. A few nights after, two negroes having started to go hunting with the same dog, and passed that way, the dog came again to the place, and having just gone out to walk about, discovered me and barked, on which thinking myself discovered, I spoke to them to beg concealment. On making myself known they fled from me. Knowing then they would betray me**, I immediately left my hiding place, and was pursued almost incessantly **until I was taken a fortnight afterwards by Mr. Benjamin Phipps, in a little hole I had dug out with my sword, for the purpose of concealment,** under the top of a fallen tree. On Mr. Phipps' discovering the place of my concealment, he cocked his gun and aimed at me. I requested him not to shoot and I would give up, upon which he demanded my sword. I delivered it to him, and he brought me to prison.

THE TRIAL OF NAT TURNER

The Commonwealth
vs.
Nat Turner.

Charged with making insurrection and plotting to take away the lives of divers free white persons, &c. on the 22d of August, 1831.

The court composed of - , having met for the trial of Nat **Turner, the prisoner was brought in and arraigned, and upon his arraignment pleaded** *Not guilty*; **saying to his counsel, that he did not feel so.**

On the part of the Commonwealth, Levi Waller was introduced, who being sworn, deposed as follows: (*agreeably to Nat's own Confession.*) Col. Trezvant was then introduced, who being sworn, narrated Nat's Confession to him, as follows: (*his Confession as given to Mr. Gray.*) The prisoner introduced no evidence, and the case was submitted without argument to the court, who having found him guilty, <u>**Jeremiah Cobb, Esq. Chairman, pronounced the sentence of the court, in the following words: "Nat Turner! Stand up. Have you anything to say why sentence of death should not be pronounced against you?**</u>

NAT TURNER

"I have not. I have made a full confession to Mr. Gray, and I have nothing more to say. I had many hair breadth escapes, which your time will not permit you to relate. I am here loaded with chains, and willing to suffer the fate that awaits me."

Jeremiah Cobb, Esq. Chairman,

"I am, nevertheless called upon to pass the sentence of the court. The time between this and your execution, will necessarily be very short; and your only hope must be in another world. The judgment of the court is, that you be taken hence to the jail from whence you came, thence to the place of execution, and on Friday next, between the hours of 10 A. M. and 2 P. M. be hung by the neck until you are dead, dead, dead and may the Lord have mercy upon your soul."

LEE CUMMINGS
A TIME TO SPEAK

"In the Government sponsored school system the so-called Negro has been taught that his fathers were slaves and yet his actions prove that he didn't view himself as a slave? **To make a decision to be free at all cost is the actions of a free man not a slave or a robot.** The man thief is hypocritical in his mental assessment of the man he stole and let me show you why. **Now check this out….the stealer of men** is holding a man, his woman and his child against their will and yet **the thief** describes this stolen man's desire to be free as **fanatical…diabolical….crazed** and **delusional**. So I asked myself the question, what is the mind of God concerning the actions of Nat Turner and the other captive men who acted in like manner? I found my answer in Exodus **(Exodus 21:16)**, verse16, "**he that steals a man and sells him or if he be found in his hand he shall surely be put to death.** "These are not the words of the prophet Moses, God is speaking and teaching Moses how to deal with a man stealer.....**Gods judgment**....kill the man thief and I agree with God! Why does God pronounce death on the man stealer? See Deuteronomy **(Deuteronomy 24:7)** verse 7 "**if a man be found stealing any of his brothers** of the children of Israel and make merchandise of him or sells him, then **the thief shall die** and **you shall put away this great evil away from among you.**" The God of the creation sees **stealing a man as an evil thing**! What happens if the thief dies while stealing? See Exodus (Exodus 22:2) verse 2, **if a thief be found breaking up and be smitten that he die**, **there shall no blood be shed for him!**

Nat Turner was judged in his generation and condemned by men who supported the institution of slavery. I want to put Nat Turner on the judgment seat again....before you.....you judge Nat Turner. The courts in America are given guidelines on how to try a case and I am going to give you guidelines; I want you to apply the statutes of God to Nat Turners case; use the scriptures that I have quoted above. If you are a teacher in a classroom why not give this exercise to the class...it should make for a great discussion.

NEW YORK SLAVE REBELLION 1712
ARTICLE BY CLAUDIA SUTHERLAND

Between twenty-five and fifty blacks congregated at midnight in **New York City, New York** on April 6, 1712. With guns, swords and knives in hand. The slaves first set fire to an outhouse then fired shots at several white slave owners, who had raced to the scene to fight the fire. By the end of the night, nine whites were killed and six whites were injured. The next day the governor of New York ordered the New York and Westchester militias to "drive the island." With the exception of six rebels who committed suicide before they were apprehended, **all of the rebels were captured and punished with ferocity ranging from being burned alive, to being broken by a wheel.** The swift punishment of the guilty was not enough to quell the concerns of slave owners and their political body. Within months, the New York Assembly passed "an act for preventing, suppressing and punishing the conspiracy and insurrection of Negroes and other slaves." Masters were permitted to punish their slaves at their full discretion, "not extending to life or member." Even the manumission of New York slaves was deterred by this bill; masters were required to pay two hundred pounds security to the government and a twenty-pound annuity to the freed slave. Despite these stringent laws, New York would escape slave rebellion for only twenty-nine years.

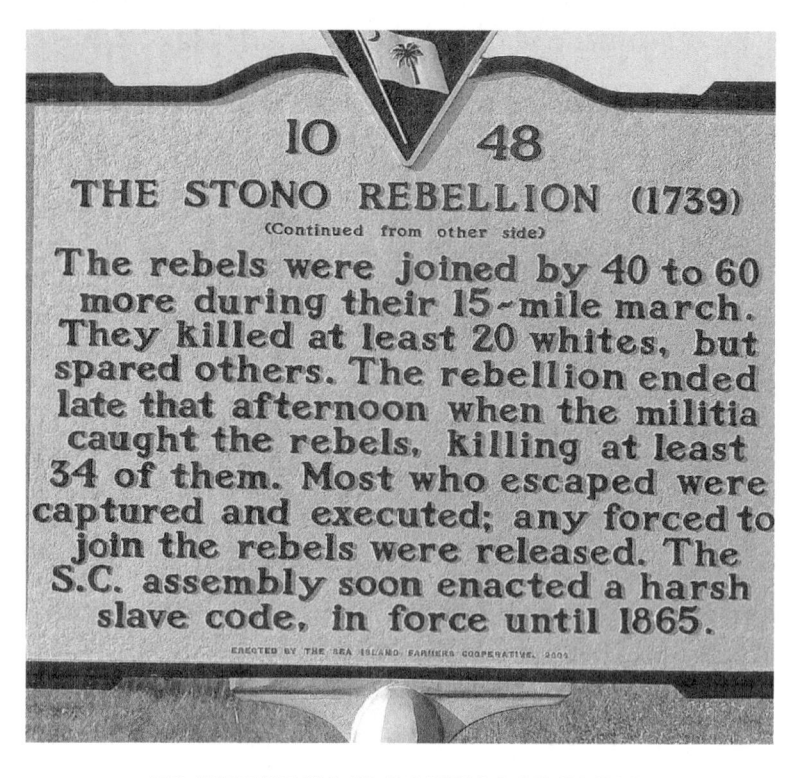

> **10 48**
> **THE STONO REBELLION (1739)**
> (Continued from other side)
> The rebels were joined by 40 to 60 more during their 15-mile march. They killed at least 20 whites, but spared others. The rebellion ended late that afternoon when the militia caught the rebels, killing at least 34 of them. Most who escaped were captured and executed; any forced to join the rebels were released. The S.C. assembly soon enacted a harsh slave code, in force until 1865.

US HIGHWAY 17-SOUTH CAROLINA

The Stono Rebellion was a slave rebellion that began on 9 September 1739, in the colony of South Carolina. It was the largest slave uprising in the British mainland colonies, with 25 white people and 35 to 50 black people killed. The uprising was led by native Africans who were likely from the Central African Kingdom of Congo, as some of the rebels spoke Portuguese. Their leader, Jemmy, was a literate slave. In some reports, **however, he is referred to as "Cato",** and likely was held by the Cato, or Cater, family who lived near the Ashley River and north of the Stono River. He led 20 other enslaved Congolese, who may have been former soldiers, in an armed march south from the Stono River (for which the rebellion is named). They were bound for Spanish Florida. This was due to a Spanish effort to destabilize British rule, where they (the Spanish) had promised freedom and land at St. Augustine to slaves who escaped from the British colonies. The timeline of the Louisiana Purchase suggests that this argument is a lie....Britain didn't purchase the slave States until 1803! Jemmy and his group recruited nearly 60 other slaves and killed some whites before being intercepted and defeated by South Carolina militia near the Edisto River. A group of slaves escaped and traveled another 30 miles (50 km) before battling a week later with the militia. Most of the captured slaves were executed. **Executed for the notion of being free...can't let this kind of Negro live!**

Take careful notice of the **Narrative....the slaves revolted....the slaves escaped....the slaves were executed.....**use your brain. These are not the actions of a slave or the actions of a robot....these are the actions of free men! The whites couldn't understand why the **propaganda/brainwashing** did not work on these men who had been held captive. <u>**Your condition does not define you**</u>.....what people think of you does not define you....it is your perception of self....**how you see yourself that defines you....how do you see yourself**?

The Government sponsored education that our children receive in the United States subconsciously teaches our children that the so-called Negro was a willing participant in his captivity. Real history proves that this is absurd and a lie....the Negro fought to the death to be free. Think about this for one moment....the only reason the captives in the South were freed is because the blacks resisted the narrative....**"that the blacks were slaves"**, they never bought into this abominable thought...they knew who they were and they made sure their children knew of their former state as free beings. Think about this...will a slave runaway, kill his master, and jump overboard a slave ship in the Atlantic Ocean...with Sharks following the ship? A slave won't starve himself, a slave won't poison his kidnapper, a slave won't' take his own life rather than be enslaved....these are the actions of a free man...not a slave! This is nothing but brainwashing and it began from the time that our fathers were children. This racist kidnapper was trying to break the will of our fathers before they could walk or talk! In a very subtle way this is happening everyday to our children in the Government sponsored school system....this is the reason our children don't want to go to school...they are tired of hearing about white supremacy! They are trying to escape the mental damage that is being inflicted on them 365 days a year. They have to sit in the classroom and hear someone call their ancestors slaves! If you have no other choice but to send your child to these institutions then make sure you teach him the truth about himself! It is time to hear the real Harriet Tubman story.....get ready!

HARRIET TUBMAN ROSS STEWART-LIBRARY OF CONGRESS

After Harriet Tubman escaped slavery she completed 13 missions **rescuing her family** and other members of the Negro race from the hard captivity in America. She was nicknamed Moses and large rewards were issued for her arrest and whereabouts but they had no knowledge that it was her! This is the legend of the Underground Railroad. There is a lesson in her **(Harriet Tubman)** actions and that is when you make it out of the ghetto don't forget to reach back and help the ones left behind! I would be remiss **if I didn't mention the true white Christians in history who helped the Negro captive** going against the cruel ideology of that generation. The news clipping to the right of

Harriet Tubman is a news article about her and her 2 brothers running away and the reward for their capture and return. What if I told you that you have never heard the real **Harriet Tubman Ross Stewart** story and that until today it has been a secret? **The question is....what was Harriet really up to?** The answer to this **riddle** can be found in the last names of the people that Harriett Tubman Ross Stewart rescued. Look carefully at the last names on this list.

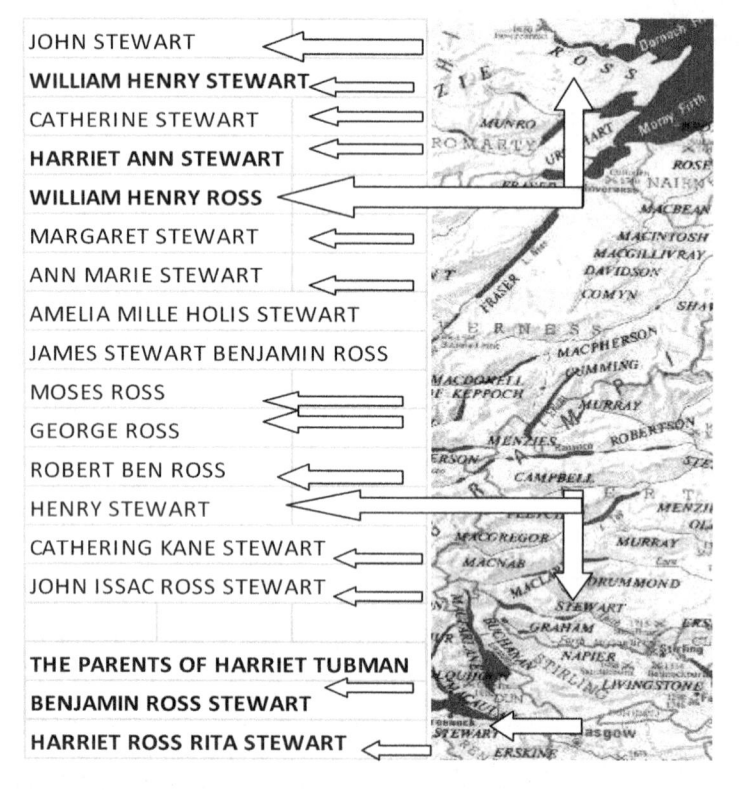

JOHN STEWART
WILLIAM HENRY STEWART
CATHERINE STEWART
HARRIET ANN STEWART
WILLIAM HENRY ROSS
MARGARET STEWART
ANN MARIE STEWART
AMELIA MILLE HOLIS STEWART
JAMES STEWART BENJAMIN ROSS
MOSES ROSS
GEORGE ROSS
ROBERT BEN ROSS
HENRY STEWART
CATHERING KANE STEWART
JOHN ISSAC ROSS STEWART
THE PARENTS OF HARRIET TUBMAN
BENJAMIN ROSS STEWART
HARRIET ROSS RITA STEWART

I researched Harriet's parent's last names; Stewart and Ross....I found out that they were Scottish. I grabbed a medieval Scottish clan's map and I found out that they were Royalty from the Highlands of Scotland. Now my curiosity was peaked, so I sought eyewitness accounts (descriptions) as to the color of the Highlanders of Scotland. **Brace yourself ...this is unbelievable.**

EYEWITNESS DESCRIPTION OF THE HIGHLANDERS OF SCOTLAND

PROFESSOR BOYD DAWKINS

PROF. BOYD DAWKINS 1837-1929

BRITISH GEOLOGIST, ARCHAEOLOGIST, ESSAY; OUR EARLIEST ANCESTORS PAGE 96 & 97

"**In the year 449 A.D certain Englishmen came from North Germany and the Southern shores of the Baltic sea** and pushed the Britain's (ancient name of England) westward. By the year 607 A.D, the English had pushed the Britain's westward as far as Chester. "**The English** carved out **Yorkshire, Chester and Southern Lancashire forming the Kingdom of Northumbria."Professor Boyd Dawkins is giving the location of the whites in England.** THEY ARE NOT FROM THE CAUCUS MOUNTAINS!

"The inhabitants of Britain belong to very different races; Britain was inhabited by the **Basque** from ancient times and **they called themselves Roman citizens**. In their books they were called the Britain's or Welsh; there are two type of Welsh, one is **dark and 5 feet 4 inches** and the other is **tall and round headed**. "The **English pushed the Dark Welsh/Britain Westward into** Wales, Cumberland, Westmoreland, **Highlands of Scotland,** Cornwall and Devon."

Professor Dawkins is telling the reader that the original inhabitants of England and Britain were black. He is also letting the reader know that **the blacks were pushed into Britain, Wales and the Highlands of Scotland!** He is telling us that Britain and England was originally black before the white barbarian invasion (449 A.D). The Lord has given us the first clues....the Highlanders of Scotland were **a black people**....are there anymore eyewitnesses? Yes...let's bring Benjamin Franklin to the witness stand. Professor Dawkins said," his father's came from North of Germany by the Southern Shores of the Baltic Sea. Let's see what Benjamin Franklin has to say about this statement.

SEE THE EYEWITNESS TESTIMONY OF BENJAMIN FRANKLIN ON THE NEXT PAGE

BENJAMIN FRANKLIN ESSAY
AMERICA AS A LAND OF OPPORTUNITY-1751

"Which leads me to add one Remark: That **the Number of purely white People in the World is proportionally very small.** All Africa is black or tawny. Asia chiefly tawny. **America (exclusive of the new Comers) wholly so.** And in Europe, the Spaniards, Italians, French, Russians and Swedes, are generally of what we call a swarthy Complexion; **as are the Germans also,** the Saxons only excepted, who with the English, make the principal Body of White People on the Face of the Earth!!!

Benjamin Franklin said," the Germans were swarthy/black **except....the Saxons and English."** He is referring to the white Barbarians that Professor Boyd Dawkins told us about when he said," our fathers (whites) came from North of Germany and the Southern shores of Germany." This is what Benjamin Franklin meant when he said Germany is swarthy/black **except the Saxons and English-invaders. I will deal with the other black nations in Europe later when dealing with the colonies.**

EYEWITNESSES CONTINUED

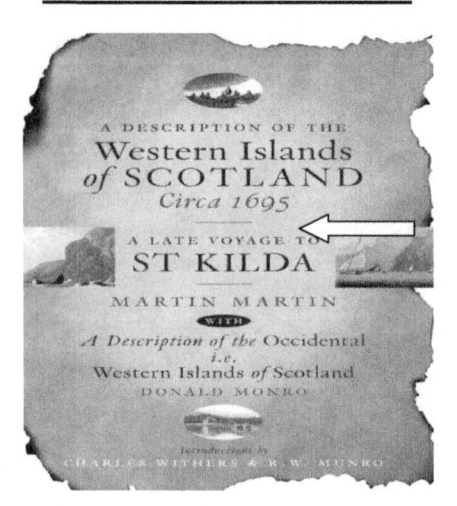

A DESCRIPTION OF <u>THE WESTERN ISLANDS OF SCOTLAND</u> CIRCA <u>1695</u> A VOYAGE TO ST KILDA, MARTIN, MARTIN

THE COMPLEXION OF THE ISLANDERS OF SKY IS BLACK.

THE COMPLEXION OF THE ISLANDERS OF ARRAN IS BROWN.

THE COMPLEXION OF THE ISLANDERS OF JURA IS BLACK.

THE COMPLEXION OF THE ISLANDERS OF THE ISLE OF COLONSAY IS BLACK.

THE COMPLEXION OF THE ISLE OF GIGHA IS BLACK.

This is not only an accurate description of the Scottish people but it is a description of the original Colonists of the 13 British colonies....this is the secret of Europe....that the original colonists were black. This eyewitness account was given in 1695...this timeline runs parallel with the founding of the colonies. I have a greater eyewitness than this. **Come and see.**

EYEWITNESS CONTINUED

MEMOIRS OF THE PUBLIC AND PRIVATE LIFE OF WILLIAM PENN

PG-140

"The natives I shall consider in <u>their persons</u>, languages, manners, customs and Governments. <u>Their complexion is black</u> but <u>**by design like the Gypsies in England**</u> and using no defense against the Sun<u>....their skin must be swarthy/black.</u>"

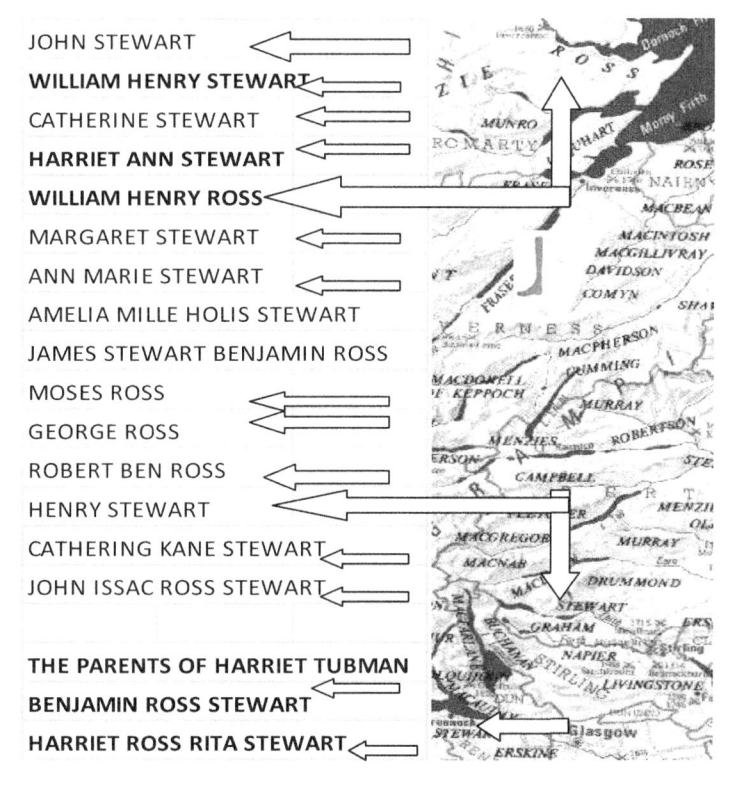

JOHN STEWART ⇐
WILLIAM HENRY STEWART ⇐
CATHERINE STEWART ⇐
HARRIET ANN STEWART ⇐
WILLIAM HENRY ROSS ⇐
MARGARET STEWART ⇐
ANN MARIE STEWART ⇐
AMELIA MILLE HOLIS STEWART
JAMES STEWART BENJAMIN ROSS
MOSES ROSS ⇐
GEORGE ROSS
ROBERT BEN ROSS ⇐
HENRY STEWART ⇐
CATHERING KANE STEWART ⇐
JOHN ISSAC ROSS STEWART ⇐

THE PARENTS OF HARRIET TUBMAN
BENJAMIN ROSS STEWART
HARRIET ROSS RITA STEWART ⇐

Why did Harriet rescue the Stewart's and Ross?

THE STEWART KINGS OF SCOTLAND WHO SAT ON THE THRONE OF ENGLAND

THEY CALLED THEMSELVES JACOBITES OR HEBREWS

IMAGE KING JAMES STEWART THE 6TH OF SCOTLAND

NATIONAL PORTRAIT GALLERY OF LONDON-1603

King James Stewart was a highlander from Scotland who also called himself a iacobvs, in Hebrew it means Jacobite, this man was an Israelite. You can find the research in the Negro Question Part 6...the 13 black colonies. This conversation that you and I are having today is a secret in these colonies. King James was known as King James Stewart the 6th of Scotland and he became King James Stewart the 1st of England. They try to hide his Scottish background because the scholars know that the Scots were a black Nation of people from ancient times.

MEMOIRS
OF THE
SECRET SERVICES
OF
JOHN MACKY, Esq;
During the REIGNS of
King WILLIAM, Queen ANNE, and King GEORGE I.
INCLUDING, ALSO,
The true SECRET HISTORY of the Rife, Promotions, &c. of the *English* and *Scots* NOBILITY; Officers, Civil, Military, Naval, and other Perfons of Diftinction, from the REVOLUTION. In their refpective CHARACTERS at large; drawn up by Mr. MACKY, purfuant to the Direction of Her ROYAL HIGHNESS the Princefs SOPHIA.

KING CHARLES STEWART 1ST OF SCOTLAND AND ENGLAND-NATIONAL PORTRAIT GALLERY

PUBLISHED 1733 NICHOLS AND SONS NEW YORK LIBRARY

(1) Charles Lenos page-36,**Duke of Richmond**, <u>**son of Charles the 1st of Scotland**</u>. **Black complexion, much like King Charles.**

This is an eyewitness account of a description of King Charles the 2nd of Scotland by English Secret Service agent John Macky. He **(John Macky)** served under King William, Queen Anne and King George 1st and was ordered by the Princess Sophia to create this document. This is a government document of the highest level. Who are you going to believe?

MEMOIRS
OF THE
SECRET SERVICES
OF
JOHN MACKY, Esq;

During the REIGNS of
King WILLIAM, Queen ANNE, and
King GEORGE I.

INCLUDING, ALSO,

The true SECRET HISTORY of the Rise, Promotions, &c. of the English and Scots Nobility; Officers, Civil, Military, Naval, and other Persons of Distinction, from the REVOLUTION. In their respective CHARACTERS at large; drawn up by Mr. MACKY, pursuant to the Direction of Her ROYAL HIGHNESS the Princess SOPHIA.

KING CHARLES THE 2ND OF SCOTLAND AND ENGLAND
CHARTERS OF GUERNSEY-TIM THORNTON-2004

This is an authentic image of King Charles Stewart 2nd Below is an eyewitness account of what King Charles the 2nd and what his son looked like. The eyewitness in this matter is former English Secret Service agent John Macky!

(6) Charles **Duke of St. Albans,** page 40, **1st son of Charles the 2nd.Black complexion, much like King Charles.**

So far all of the eyewitnesses are saying the same thing; the Scottish people were a black and brown people.

MEMOIRS
OF THE
SECRET SERVICES
OF
JOHN MACKY, Esq;

During the REIGNS of
King WILLIAM, Queen ANNE, and King GEORGE I.

INCLUDING, ALSO,

The true SECRET HISTORY of the Rise, Promotions, &c. of the English and Scots NOBILITY; Officers, Civil, Military, Naval, and other Persons of Distinction, from the REVOLUTION. In their respective CHARACTERS at large; drawn up by Mr. MACKY, pursuant to the Direction of Her ROYAL HIGHNESS the Princess SOPHIA.

KING CHARLES THE 2ND OF SCOTLAND AND ENGLAND
RHODE ISLAND CHARTER-1636-OFFICIAL DOCUMENT

This is an authentic image of King Charles Stewart the 2nd, below is an eyewitness account of what King Charles the 2nd looked like, he and his son. The eyewitness in this matter is former English Secret Service agent John Macky!

(6) Charles **Duke of St. Albans,** page 40, **1st son of Charles the 2nd. Black complexion, much like King Charles.**

I had to parade all of these eyewitnesses before you to get your mind ready for the real Harriet Tubman Ross Stewart. Harriett Tubman Ross Stewart was a black Scottish Princess from the Royal house of Stewart. Harriet's real mission was to rescue the black Royal Stewart seed from captivity in Maryland. I have placed ships manifest of prisoners shipped into the colonies during the Jacobite rebellion of 1715 and 1745. **They rounded up the black Stewart Princes and sent them into the colonies as Prisoners!**

JACOBITE REBELLION SHIPS MANIFEST

ISAIAH 44: 5 another shall call himself by the name Jacob

The plot thickens when Harriet Tubman Ross Stewart rescues a black man from slavery named William Henry Stewart. The name **William Stewart** can be found **on the convict ship SCIPIO 1716** and the ship York.

THE ROYAL SEED OF THE STEWARTS
CONVICT SHIP SCIPIO 1716-SHIPS MANIFEST

76 ALEX STEWART
77 CHARLES STEWART
78 DANL STEWART
79 DANL STEWART
80 DANL STEWART
81 JOHN STEWART
82 JOHN STEWART
83 JOHN STEWART
84 JOHN STEWART
85 WILLIAM STEWART ⇐
12 PETER CUMMIN
13 PETER CUMMIN

The Jacobites were a group of Hebrew Israelites that tried to restore the black Scottish Stewart Kings back to the throne and hence they took on the name Jacobites. The rebellions in your history books are called the Jacobite rebellion of 1715 and 1745. Since slavery was not recognized by Britain nor England the system of indentured servitude was established....these are the so-called convicts that England sent into the colonies. The white version of history left out one small detail....**these were black Prince, Princesses and noblemen.**

(THE SHIP ELIZABETH AND ANN 1716)

*List of rebel prisoners **(Royal Seed)** imported by Capt Edwd Trafford, in

ROBT STEWART
ROBT STEWART
JNO STEWART
MALCOM STEWART
JNO STEWART
JNO STEWART

(SHIP THE GOOD SPEED 1716)

Liverpool, England to Annapolis, Maryland
18 October 1716
I am only listing the last name Stewart/Steward/Stuart that is found on the ships manifest.

PRISONER NAMES

Daniel Steward
John Stewart

This proves that the **Stewart Royals** were being rounded up and deported into the colonies as convicts. What was their crime? They believed in the divine right of Kings to rule and they tried to restore the black Stewarts to the throne of the three Kingdoms. Are you still there? Let's play the game conspiracy theory...what are the odds that the same name **William Henry Seward** appears as Secretary of State in the administration of Abraham Lincoln. Think about this, Harriet Tubman Stewart rescues a man with **the name William Henry Steward in 1854** and **11 years later this same name appears as Secretary of State of the United States, minus the-T,** what are the odds? **Are you still there?**

WILLIAM HENRY STEWARD/STEWART
WILLIAM HENRY S- EWARD/SEWART

The same day that Abraham Lincoln was assassinated **the entire family of black Stewards/Seward's** was savagely attacked by an assassin by the name of Lewis Powell, a twenty year old Confederate soldier. Powell slashed Secretary of State William Henry Seward, (Steward) Assistant Secretary of State Frederick Augustus Seward (Steward) and his daughter but they all lived! **It was a hit on the entire administration.** There is another intriguing element to this story that cannot be dismissed. <u>**When Harriet Ross Tubman and her family made it to Canada they dropped the last name, Ross (Earl) and assumed the title Stewart**</u> **(King)** this can't be a coincidence. **Check out the names.**

THE DREADED PAPAL BULLS

POPE NICHOLAS THE 5TH REIGN 1447-1455

MUSEUM-PLANTIN MORETUS

PAPAL BULL-DUM DIVERSAS

In 1452, Pope Nicholas the 5th authorized King Alfonso V of Portugal to reduce any "Saracens **(Muslims)** and pagans **(black JEWS)** and any <u>other unbelievers</u> to perpetual slavery**, thereby ushering in the West African slave trade. **The Romanus Pontifex**, also **issued by Pope Nicholas V in 1455,** <u>sanctioned the seizure of non-Christian lands, and encouraged the enslavement of non Christian people in Africa</u> and the Americas. Basically it gave the green light to "invade, search out, capture, vanquish, and subdue all non Catholics. It wasn't about religion…it was about the money and they didn't mind blaspheming the name of Jesus to get it.

POPE ALEXANDER THE VI

CORRIDOIO VASARIANO MUSEUM, FLORENCE, ITALY

The **Inter Caetera**, signed by **Pope Alexander VI in 1493**, states we **(the Papacy)** command you (Spain) ... <u>**to instruct the aforesaid inhabitants and residents and dwellers therein in the Catholic faith**</u>, and train them in good morals." This papal law sanctioned and paved the way for European colonization and Catholic missions in the New World. Who were the non believers? **Remember the Ashanti, the Igbo's (Jews of Nigeria), Beta Jews of Ethiopia, the Falaysha Jews, the Lemba tribe, Jews in the wheat coast, the gold coast and the Kingdom of Judah. These people worshipped the God of the Sabbath; they** circumcised their sons on the 8th day, they kept the dietary law, they kept the blowing of trumpets and the feast days. **The people of the captivity were non believers of what?** Examine the verbiage from the council of the Laodicea, it states," that Christians **must not Judaize by resting on the Sabbath day but must work on that day**, rather honoring the Lords day (Sunday) (which Lord?) if they be found resting as Christians; but if any should be found to be Judaizers let them be anathema from Christ! **This is one of the reasons why the Europeans justified enslaving the black Hebrews from West Africa because they were Judaizers!!** After all of these official documents coming from the Angle, Saxon, and Jute priests (Papacy) you have a strange event taking place in 1865. Remember under **the law of darkness**, it was illegal to teach the Negro to read or write, so who do you suppose made his way to the so called slave quarters to instruct the Negro in the ways of Christ? Remember the Negro couldn't read or write under the laws of darkness, so who do you think taught the Negro his religion? It was the Pope and his crew...the same organization that enslaved the Negro.**This is why the Lord had the prophet to write this people has been robbed and spoiled;** robbed of his memory, his identity, his resting place and his God! The most high had it written in the writings of the prophet Moses (Deuteronomy 32:36), that when he saw that Israel's power was gone he would intervene and he did. Watch God in action, the Negro in the South didn't have an army to fight on his behalf so the Lord of the Sabbath made the North and the South fight each other. This happens to be one of the Lords calling cards to make your enemies fight each other, go with me to a scene in the Bible. You will need to read the entire 20th chapter of 2nd Chronicles but I shall narrate for you. A great host came up against Jehoshaphat and Judah which caused the Nation to cry to God for help. The Bible says that the spirit of God came over the priest Azariah instructing him that the Lord would fight this battle for Judah. In the 20th chapter of 2nd Chronicles verse 23 it reads," for the children of Ammon and Moab stood up against the inhabitants of mount Seir utterly to slay and destroy them; **when they made an end of the inhabitants of Seir, every one helped to destroy one another!** This is what happened in the American Civil war....the Lord had the two brothers...the North and the South to destroy one another so that the brothers in the South could go free. The Lord remembered his covenant with Abraham in which he said," I will be a God unto your seed that shall come after you." This was the Lords doing and it was marvelous in his eyes and yet....no man has considered it.

EMANCIPATION PROCLAMATION - 1865

LIBRARY OF CONGRESS

Before Abraham Lincoln issued his emancipation proclamation over 250,000 free black soldiers had fought on the side of the North to free the enslaved blacks in the South. U.S history does not deal kindly to the free Negros in the North because it appears that **the free Negros history has been destroyed.** Let's do some basic math.....the historians say that 250,000 free blacks fought in the civil war....let's give each man a wife and 5 children...that would give me a population of over **one million free blacks inhabiting the North.** Contrary to what you have been taught the original colonists of the 13 colonies were black Scots, Black Brits, black Irish, black Germans and black Swedes. These men have always been free and were never enslaved....so what is my point. The first point is that after the civil war the free Negro soldiers went back North and my second point is one of great significance....you have millions of Negros walking around America that have always been free.....never captive! **The narrative that is taught in the Government sponsored school system is that every Negro in America is the descendant of a slave;** the narrative is a lie....and **we reject the narrative.** This is the first time in modern history that the Negro question had arisen and believe it or not the Negro started the question **(you mean to tell me this Negro can think?** History records that three Presidents tried to answer the Negro question; President Monroe, **Lincoln, and Jackson.** President James Monroe had **$100,000 in gold** appropriated for the migration of Negroes to Liberia. Lincoln worked the hardest on the emigration of the Negro, **Lincoln tried to secure land in South America but three nations vetoed the effort; Nicaragua, Honduras and Costa Rica.**

ARTICLE THE GUARDIAN NEWSPAPER JAN-2019

Hundreds of Central American migrants have continued their march towards the United States, crossing from **Honduras into Guatemala,** as Donald Trump again demanded the construction of a border wall he claims would keep such groups out. **Nicaragua began its march in 2018.**

These same Nations had no compassion...**zilch**...for the so-called Negro when he was trying to find a suitable habitation among the Nations. These same Nations find themselves in the same position; howbeit their plight is economical and sometimes political. This is why the second great commandment is important...**to love your neighbor as yourself**...because you never know when you will need to be loved!

FREDERICK DOUGLAS,1818-1895, BLACK ABOLITIONIST
NATIONAL ARCHIVES AND RECORDS

Frederick Douglas took a delegation of Negro elders to see Lincoln about the emigration issue, and stated unequivocally that the Negro was here to stay. You might not like this but I am curious.... who gave Frederick Douglas the right to speak for 4 to 5 million captive people? It has been recorded that at least 14,000 freed blacks had sent in letters expressing their intent to relocate if given the opportunity. **I am forever indebted to President Lincoln for**

one thing; in his communications he defined the Negro in Americas as a captive, not a slave. I am of the opinion that the degrading term Slave should be stricken from all history books in America. I don't mean to vilify Frederick Douglass because he has earned a seat in the Negro hall of fame; Frederick helped to speed up the emancipation of the Negro people through his agitation. It should be very apparent to you that the Negro question has yet to be answered but as you will see later I will attempt to answer this question. The God of Israel had seen enough of the carnage and wickedness associated with the North Atlantic Slave trade and he knew the secret intention of the white man concerning the Negro! If you don't remember anything that you've read in this book....don't you ever forget this one thing; the whites in America had secret intentions of making the Negro a perpetual slave for life! Perpetual slavery was mentioned in the Willie Lynch letters and the Papal Bulls; Dum Diversa and the Romanus Pontifex. So after all of the slave revolts and wars the Government finally got around to granting the Negro in the South his sovereign right....freedom. If you go back and look at history the Negro was thrust out of the plantations onto the streets of the South. He was not given reparations and had no land to till. The beast of burden, **the Negro**, was thrust out into the streets of the South. He was sent out of Pharaohs house without an education; he could not read or write. The Emancipation Proclamation made 5 million Negros homeless in the United States of America. The so-called Negro was forced back onto the plantation to work as a sharecropper. The Emancipation Proclamation strengthened the hands of the Negro exploiters because the only thing the Negro could do was purchase...he had nothing to sell. **The fix was in**...the Negro couldn't read or write and he owned nothing; he was set up to be exploited again. Let us take our leave from this subject for one precious moment so that you can see the original colonists of the 13 British colonies were black.

CHAPTER 6   THE 13 BLACK BRITISH COLONIES

I shall prove to you that the 13 British colonies were colonized by the black Scottish/Britain's. In order for me to accomplish this I must borrow from the work of Helen Ainslie Smith.

HELEN AINSIE SMITH

THE THIRTEEN COLONIES PART 1, PAGE-386

"In the year 1664 there **were 7000 Dutchmen, besides the real Dutch; Prussians, Bohemians, French, Swedes, Norwegians, Danes and 5000 English including Scots, Welsh and Irish.**

Is there an eyewitness that can tell me what these **7000 Dutchmen, besides the real Dutch; Prussians, Bohemians, French, Swedes, Norwegians, Danes and 5000 English including Scots, Welsh and Irish looked like? Yes come and see.**

BENJAMINS FRANKLINS ESSAY-1751

AMERICA AS A LAND OF OPPORTUNITY

"The **Spaniards, Italians, French, Russians and Swedes, are generally of what we call a swarthy/BLACK Complexion; as are the Germans also." Except the Saxons!**

This is creepy right? All of the nations that Helen said were in the colonies were black nations....is there more? **Yes come and see.**

BENJAMIN FRANKLIN

WHAT POLITENESS DEMANDED, ETHNIC OMISSIONS IN FRANKLINS AUTOBIOGRAPHY PG-290

MARC L HARRIS –PENN STATE UNIVERSITY

THE WORDS OF DOCTOR ALEXANDER HAMILTON PENNSYLVANIA 1744

"I dined at a tavern with a very mixed company of different nations; there were **Scots, Germans, Irish, Dutch, Roman Catholics and Jews.**

Did you see that ….these same black people that Benjamin described as being black were the colonists dining in a tavern together…..is there further proof? **Come and see.**

BENJAMIN FRANKLIN AND THE BLACK FRENCH
MEMOIRS OF THE LIFE AND WRITINGS OF BENJAMIN FRANKLIN PG-310

"On the road yesterday (in France) traveling to Nantes, we met six or seven country women in company on horseback and astride. Most of the men have good complexions, not **swarthy/black** like those **in North France** and Abbeville."

Benjamin Franklin was the American Ambassador to France and lived there for 9 years….his account of the black French is that of an eyewitness. I have another eyewitness, **come and see.**

MEMOIRS OF THE STORMING OF THE BASILLE IN FRANCE
THOMAS JEFFERSON

"I saw 60,000 Frenchman of all colors."

What we are looking at is one of the greatest cover-ups in human history. Not only have we been herded into their schools but they have done that which only the false prophet is capable of doing. It is written in Daniel (Daniel 7:25) Verse 25 and he shall speak great words against the most high and shall wear out the saints of the most high **and think to change times!**

The changing of times is the rewriting of history; this is exactly what the current Europeans have done to the real history of the 13 colonies. They have blotted out the black man's history and replaced it with lies; is there more? **Come and see.**

THE BLACK ASSEMBLY OF THE 13 COLONIES
WHAT POLITENESS DEMANDED, ETHNIC OMISSIONS IN
FRANKLINS AUTOBIOGRAPHY PG-294
CONTINUED ON THE NEXT PAGE

THE BLACK ASSEMBLY OF THE 13 COLONIES
WHAT POLITENESS DEMANDED, ETHNIC OMISSIONS IN FRANKLINS AUTOBIOGRAPHY PG-294

"**Two other ethnic references defy classification**, in one case Franklins narrator is trading quips with political opponents about **whether the assembly's members resembled black slaves enough** to be sold for refusing the Governors orders!

The color of the assembly men was never questioned...they agreed that they were black but this opens another door....how could slaves write laws? They couldn't read or write...**so we must be talking about the original colonists who governed the colonies.** Is this it...or can I present more proof that the original colonists were black people? **Come and see.**

WILLIAM PENN DESCRIBING THE AMERICAN INDIANS
MEMOIRS OF THE PUBLIC AND PRIVATE LIFE OF WILLIAM PENN PG-140

"The natives (Indians) I shall describe in their persons, languages, manners, customs, and Governments. **Their complexion is black but by design like the Gypsies in England** and using no defense against the sun their **skin must be swarthy.**

William Penn is describing the American Indian as a black man and comparing them to the black Europeans; what does that have to do with the colonists? **Come and see.**

A JOURNAL OF A TOUR TO THE SCOTTISH HEBRIDES WITH SAMUEL JOHNSON, AUTHOR JAMES BOSWELL-PUBLISHED 1785 &1810, ACCURATE ACCOUNT PAGE-123

"There was great diversity in the faces of the circle around us; **some were as black and wild in their appearance as any American savage (Indian) whatever.**

The man said," the black Scots were as black as any Indian he had ever seen." This statement comes within 2 years of the Paris Peace Treaty signed by King George the 3rd. The author called the Islands of Scotland the Hebrides....is this not slang for Hebrew? Do you mean the original colonists were Hebrews? Yes...can I prove this...yes? **Come and see.**

HISTORICAL SKETCHES A COLLECTION OF PAPERS VOLUME 2, PAGE-226

"Several **Hessian** prisoners **(black Germans)** had been brought to Philadelphia. One of them accidently met **a settler who happened to be his first cousin,** who asked him what induced him to come to America to injure his own flesh and blood? Others being asked said the English officer made them to think that the colonists were savages **especially those who had fringes on."**

The Hessian soldier was a black German which means that the settler-colonist had to be black. No one on Earth wears fringes on their garments but the Israelites of the Bible. This conversation plus the ships manifests prove that the original colonists had Hebrews among them in great numbers. Can I give you just a little more...just one more piece of proof? Yes...**come and see.**

THE JOURNAL OF PRIVATE DANIEL FLOHR
THE BATTLE OF YORKTOWN

"Three days later on the morning of October 18, the articles of capitulation of the English army (black Germans) in Yorktown was signed. **The defeated army marched out that afternoon and the Royal Deux Ponts, German/French** held the place of honor among the French troops present. Afterward the troops were freed to inspect the damage they had inflicted. Flohr was horrified; everywhere dead bodies lay around unburied they were **mohren-black.**

The word mohren comes from the word moor which simply means black. Private Flohr said that all the dead were Mohren so then....what armies were present at Yorktown? The **French, Germans,** Haitians, Indians and the....**colonists-Continental army!** Benjamin Franklin told us that the French, Germans and Indians were swarthy; the other histories that we examined proved that the original colonists were a black people. The writings of the ancient and medieval historians is not the problem; the problem is with this modern historian...he is a liar and the truth is not in him.

KING JAMES   KING CHARLES 1ST   KING CHARLES 2ND

KING WILLIAM-DUKE OF YORK   KING GEORGE 3RD-GERMAN KING

1607-VIRGINIA FOUNDED BY BLACK SCOTTISH KING JAMES THE 6TH OF SCOTLAND
1620-MASS-MAINE FOUNDED BY BLACK SCOTTISH KING JAMES THE 6TH OF SCOTLAND
1620-NEW ENGLAND FOUNDED BY BLACK SCOTTISH KING JAMES THE 6TH OF SCOTLAND

1629-NEW HAMPSHIRE FOUNDED BY BLACK SCOTTISH KING CHARLES 1ST OF SCOTLAND
1632-MARYLAND FOUNDED BY BLACK SCOTTISH KING CHARLES 1ST OF SCOTLAND

1636-RHODE ISLAND FOUNDED BY BLACK SCOTTISH KING CHARLES 2ND OF SCOTLAND
1636-CONNETICUT FOUNDED BY BLACK SCOTTISH KING CHARLES 2ND OF SCOTLAND
1638-DELAWARE FOUNDEB BY BLACK SCOTTISH KING CHARLES 2ND OF SCOTLAND
1663-NORTH CAROLINA FOUND BY BLACK SCOTTISH KING CHARLES 2ND OF SCOTLAND
1663-SOUTH CAROLINA FOUNDED BY BLACK SCOTTISH KING CHARLES 2ND OF SCOTLAND
1681-PENNSYLVANIA FOUNDED BY BLACK SCOTTISH KING CHARLES 2ND OF SCOTLAND

1664-NEW JERSEY FOUNDED BY BLACK SCOTTISH KING JAMES 2ND DUKE OF YORK
1732-GEORGIA FOUNDED BY BLACK GERMAN KING GEORGE THE GERMAN HANOVER

The Stewart Kings self styled themselves as Jacobites being interpreted....Israelites. The black Scots, Brits and black Irish were Hebrew Israelites which was proven by the fringes worn by the black Scottish colonists. If you want to know more about this subject you are going to have to purchase the Negro Question parts 6, The 13 Black Colonies and the Negro Question Part 7, the Swarthy Memoirs. **It's time for a mini recap**; we began this journey in Mesopotamia around 3500 B.C. We walked the black Mesopotamians, **who became the Hebrew Israelites**, through time **from Mesopotamia, to West Africa and now to the 13 colonies.** We have looked at the Kingdom of Judah and the Ashanti (Levites) that were being held as captives in the South. I resurrected the history of the original black Scottish colonists that the Europeans had destroyed. What if I told you that a black armed militia occupied the Eastern seaboard of the 13 British colonies during the American Revolution....would you believe me? This is another great secret of this Government and I shall show it to you from the eyes of the eyewitness!

CHAPTER 7 BLACK TROOPS OCCUPY THE 13 COLONIES

In order for you to be able to wrap your mind around this hidden truth, that a black army occupied the 13 British colonies during the American Revolution, I am going to have to bring Benjamin Franklins essay into this discussion. Benjamin Franklin wrote an essay in 1751 that the Government sponsored Universities and their scholars avoid as if it were the plague.

BENJAMIN FRANKLINS ESSAY 1751
AMERICA AS A LAND OF OPPORTUNITY
LIBRARY OF CONGRESS

"And since <u>Detachments</u> of English **from Britain sent to America, will have their Places at Home so soon supplied and increase so largely here**; who will shortly be so numerous as **to** <u>Germanize</u> us instead of our Anglifying them, and will never adopt our Language or Customs, **any more than they can acquire our Complexion. All** <u>Africa</u> **is black or tawny.** <u>Asia</u> **chiefly tawny.** <u>America</u> **(exclusive of the new Comers)** <u>wholly so.</u> **In Europe the** <u>Spaniards, Italians, French, Russians and Swedes, are generally of what we call a swarthy Complexion; as are the Germans also.</u> Swarthy was a medieval word for black.

This is an official document that you can find in the Library of Congress (Digital) written by the hand of the illustrious Benjamin

Franklin. This document gives a truthful description of the World in 1751 and Benjamin Franklin informs the reader that at this time Europe still had black ruling Nations. Franklin said," Spain, Italy, France, Russia, Swedes and Germany were **SWARTHY or black. Benjamin Franklin was crying foul….he said" detachments (an army) of Englishmen were on their way to the 13 colonies to put down the civil unrest….but they were not Englishmen.** When the British colonies in America rebelled a decade later, **several German-speaking states contracted soldiers to the British Army.** Although the leasing of soldiers to a foreign power was controversial to some Europeans, the people of these continental states generally took great pride in their soldiers' service in the war. **In some instances, <u>ethnic Germans</u> even enlisted directly into British units,** such as the 60th Regiment of Foot.

The Hessian Mercenary State Ideas, Institutions, and Reform under Frederick II, 1760-1785 (2003). The mercenaries of Hesse were very well trained and equipped; they fought well for whoever was paying their prince. At the conclusion of the war, Congress offered incentives—especially free farmland—for **<u>these ethnic Germans to remain in the United States.</u>**

The establishment has no problem telling you that the German Hessian's was the army that they sent over but they have a problem telling you that **this was a black German army.**

BLACK GERMAN DUKE, GEORGE WILLIAM 1591-1699
COUNT PALATINE <u>OF THE RHINE</u>, ZWEIBRUCKEN BIRKENFIELD
WIKEPEDIA ENCYCLOPEDIA & BIRKENFIELD HISTORY 2

Do you remember what Benjamin Franklin said? Benjamin Franklin said, **"<u>Detachments</u>** of English<u>, supplied by the Germans who don't have our complexion</u> and Germany is swarthy. What does detachments of English...<u>supplied by the Germans</u> mean? In Negro, detachments of English supplied by the Germans means, the flag that the army rides under is English but the soldiers are the hired black Hessian German army! This is what the Germans looked like in 1591.

FREDERICK 2 –GERMAN- AUSTRIAN NATIONAL LIBRARY

The Landgraviate of Hessen-Kassel, under Frederick II, an <u>uncle of King George III</u>, initially provided over 12,000 soldiers to fight in the Americas.

This is what I have been trying to tell you, **King George was a black German King from the house of Hanover.** Benjamin Franklin told the truth when he said the Germans were a black people but the historians in this generation refuse to listen!

Like their British allies, the Hessians had some difficulty acclimating themselves to North America; <u>the first troops to arrive suffered from widespread illness, which forced a delay in the attack on Long Island.</u> From 1776 on, **Hessian soldiers (black Germans) were incorporated into the British Army serving in North America**, and they fought in most of the major battles, including those of New York and New Jersey campaign, the Battle of Germantown, the Siege of Charleston and the final Siege of Yorktown where about 1,300 Germans **(black Germans)** were taken prisoner, although various reports indicate that the Germans were in better spirits than their British counterparts. It has been estimated that **Hessen-Kassel contributed over 16,000** troops (16,000 black German troops) during the course of the Revolutionary War, of whom 6,500 did not return. This is what the black German Hessians looked like and it appears that the old man, Benjamin Franklin, told the truth when he said, **"the Germans are a swarthy/black race of people."** Just in case you think the author has lost his mind or is slipping, let me read you a firsthand account of the battle at Yorktown.

THE JOURNAL OF GERMAN PRIVATE DANIEL FLOHR

THE BATTLE OF YORKTOWN

AMERICAN HISTORY.ORG

"Three days later on the morning of October 13, the articles of capitulation of the English army, **black German Hessians**, was signed. Afterward the troops were free to inspect the damage that they had inflicted. Flohr was horrified....**everywhere....there were dead bodies....they were all Mohren.** Private Flohr uses the adjective Mohren...which is derived from the word Mooren or

Moor…..which was an ancient name for BLACK! Private Flohr's diary is an eyewitness account of the armies present at Yorktown. What armies fought at Yorktown? The Haitian army, **German Hessians**, French, Swedes and **Colonists/Continental army** and yet……the eyewitness (private Flohr) said they were all black! **This means that the colonists were black.** The key to understanding the genetic makeup of this army lies in the truth written in Benjamin Franklin's essay, 1751. **"The English are sending an army supplied by the Germans who are black/swarthy and they can never acquire our complexion."**

THE ORIGINAL DRAFT OF THE DECLARATION OF INDEPENDENCE

LIBRARY OF CONGRESS-THOMAS JEFERSON

"They (Great Britain) are sending over Scotch and **foreign mercenaries** to invade and deluge us in blood."

Thomas Jefferson called them," foreign mercenaries," and Benjamin Franklin said," this army detachment that was on the way was Swarthy/black and German.

Based on the testimony of Jefferson and Franklin we are able to see thru a murky glass; we now know that **the black Scottish army** and the **black German army** occupied the 13 British colonies! This modern historian has embarked on a, "blot out campaign," anybody that's not white gets blotted out of Colonial history.

BLACK GERMAN HESSIAN ARMY OCCUPY 13 COLONIES

DESTRUCTION OF NEW YORK-CINCINATTI MUSEUM

This image is called the destruction of the statue royal in New York. Take a close look at the images because these are not slaves...**these are the black Germans** destroying a statue of King George the 3rd...the black German Hanover King of England!

120

BRITISH COMMANDER-WILLIAM HOWE-GETTY IMAGES

The American Revolution 100, the battles people and events of the American Revolution, page-58

"Commander William Howe was swarthy/black, 6 feet tall with bad teeth?

British commander William Howe **(black Brit)** with **black German Hessian troops** marched into New York in 1775 and <u>**occupied the city for 6 years**</u>. Remember what Benjamin Franklin said," the Germans are swarthy/black and that the English army is really German. The black German army was hired by the English crown and riding under the English flag. **The eyewitness description of Commander William Howe is that he was a black man.** The words of Professor Boyd Dawkins have taken hold of this book when he said;" <u>**the Britain's are a black people**</u>." **BLACK GERMANS OCCUPY NEW YORK 6 YEARS.**

THE BURNING OF CHARLESTOWN 1775

NATIONAL ARCHIVES AND RECORDS LIBRARY OF CONGRESS

In 1780 British General Cornwallis and the black German Hessian army invade and occupy Charleston Massachusetts.
BLACK GERMANS OCCUPY CHARLESTON 2 AND ½ YEARS.

BLACK GERMAN DRUMMER-ERSTES REGIMENT-BROWN UNIVERSITY

BLACK GERMAN/ENGLISH TROOPS LAND IN BOSTON

In the year 1768 the British sent 4,000 contracted black German troops into Boston to police the city after their revolt to the Townsend Act. The Townshend Acts were a series of measures, passed by the British Parliament in 1767, that taxed goods imported to the American colonies. The Colonists objected because they felt that they were being taxed without representation….sounds familiar doesn't it? Benjamin Franklin said they were swarthy Germans and Thomas Jefferson said they were foreign Mercenaries.

BOSTON MASSACRE 1770-ENGRAVER-PAUL REVERE

LIBRARY OF CONGRESS

This image was engraved by Paul Revere who had an engraving business and was contracted by the United States Government. Take a closer look at the red coats (black Germans), the English soldiers are black but remember the ethnic makeup of this army included the black Scots and black Germans. This depiction of the English army by Paul Revere is consistent with the eyewitness account of Benjamin Franklin, Thomas Jefferson and Private Daniel Flohr....the Germans were Swarthy and Moor.

BLACK GERMAN OCCUPATION OF BOSTON 7 YEARS.

BLACK OCCUPATION OF BRANDYWINE PHILADELPHIA

BLACK GERMAN HESSIAN LANDGRAVE-MORITZ HESSE-1596
IMAGE- THE CHRISTENING OF LADY ELIZABETH HESSE

BAVARIAN STATE LIBRARY

The British occupied Philadelphia from September 1778 to June 1778, exactly 10 months. The English army was led by General Cornwallis and black German Hessian General Wilhelm Knyphausen. The establishment is hiding the Hessian pictures.
BLACK GERMAN OCCUPATION OF PHILADELPHIA 10 MONTHS.

BLACK OCCUPATION OF SAVANNA GEORGIA

In the year 1778 the English led by LT. Colonel Archibald Campbell led an invasion of Savanna Georgia with an army of contracted black German Hessian troops. Colonel Archibald was a Scottish landowner from the Highlands of Scotland and what did Professor Boyd Dawkins tell us about the Highlanders? He said that they were black/swarthy. **There were four black armies present at the battle of Savanna Georgia; Haiti, France, Germany and the colonists.** I have a ships manifest from the Liverpool, a ship used to transport Jacobite rebels in 1745 that gives an accurate description of the Campbell's. **BLACK GERMAN OCCUPATION OF SAVANNA GEORGIA 4 YEARS.**

SHIPS MANIFEST THE VETERAN 1745

JACOBITE GLEANINGS FROM STATE MANUSCRIPTS

PAGES 37-48

ARTHUR J. MACBETH FORBES HARVARD COLLEGE LIBRARY

DOUGALL CAMPBELL 18 BROWN COMPLEXION

ALEXANDER CAMPBELL 18 BROWN POCK PITTED

BLACK OCCUPATION OF RHODE ISLAND

The British invaded Rode Island (1778) under the command of General Richard Prescott and General Clinton. This is probably getting to be old news to you but....the black German Hessian army was the English army that invaded Rhode Island. The general of record for the Continental army was General John Sullivan from New Hampshire. Below is a description of this black colonist **(Continental General)**.

MEMOIRS OF HENRY ARMITT BROWN

TOGETHER WITH 4 HISTORICAL ORATIONS PG-330

A DESCRIPTION OF GENERAL JOHN SULLIVAN

"Swarthy John Sullivan, a little headstrong but brave as a lion."

You must remember that John Sullivan is a colonist first and then a soldier second. This Continental **(colonist)** officer is described as a black man...swarthy means black! I told you that the original colonists were a black Scottish people. **BLACK GERMAN OCCUPATION OF RHODE ISLAND 3 YEARS.**

LIST OF BLACK COLONIST-CONTINENTAL OFFICERS

MEMOIRS OF HENRY ARMITT BROWN

TOGETHER WITH FOUR ORACLE ORATIONS PG-329

(1) GENERAL MUHLENBERG

"At the corner of the entrenchments **by the river is the Virginia Brigade of Muhlenberg....wears the buff and blue of a brigadier, his stalwart form and swarthy/black face.**"

(2) BRIGIDIER GENERAL FRANCIS MARION PG-329

"Marion was a stranger to the officers and men and they flocked about him to obtain a sight of their future commander," **he was rather below stature, lean** and Swarthy/black."

(3) CAPTAIN PAUL JONES

MEMOIRS OF THE MARQUEE OF ROCKINHAM AND HIS CONTEMPORARIES, VOL 2, PG-379

"An adventurer with a single ship caused an almost consternation in the North. **I mean Captain Paul Jones; this renegade from Scotland was a short thick man with coarse (nappy) hair and a swarthy complexion.**"

All of these colonists, Continental Officers, are described by the eyewitness as being Swarthy/black. So far all the research is adding up...but I have a greater witness than this. **COME AND SEE!**

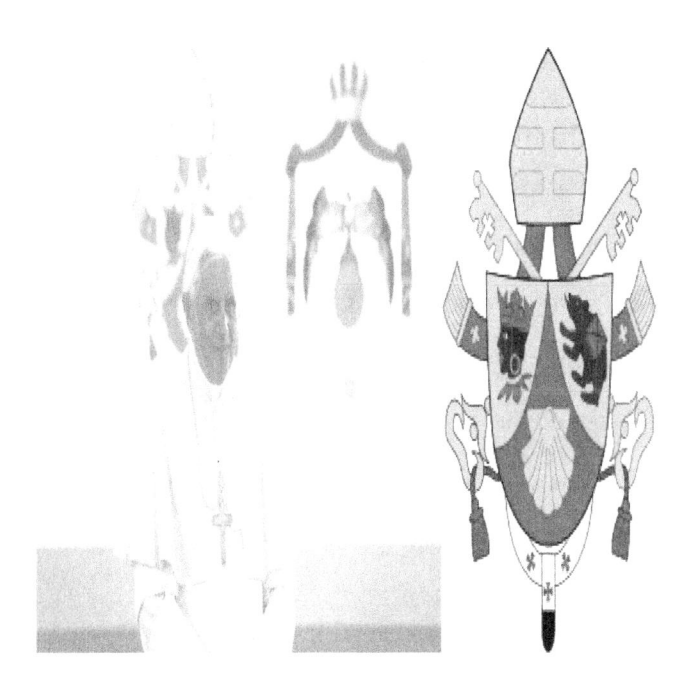

POPE RATZINGER WITH HIS BLACK GERMAN COAT OF ARMS

This is what the young people call a stunner! Are you okay? Take a moment and catch your breath….the Pope is standing in front of a medieval black German coat of Arms. What do you think? Do you think just maybe the Pope is letting you know that he knew the ancient Germans were a black people?

WHO ARE YOU GOING TO BELIEVE?

CHAPTER 8   THE QUARREL OF THE COVENANT

Do you remember ever going to the grocery store or the laundry mat with your mother and you did something or said something she didn't like? It could have been something as simple as a bad facial expression, and you got smacked right there in front of everybody, talk about being embarrassed. To strangers observing the discipline, it looked like your mother was being cruel; it was simply family business being played out in front of strangers. This is what has been going on with the so-called Negro (Hebrew Israelite) and his God over the last 2000 years. Our God and our father has been chastening his children **(the black Hebrew Israelite Nation)** in front of the global community for the breaking of his covenant. I will prove that to you with the conditions that prevailed post slavery and even down to this generation, **it was.... and still is... family business!** The living God came down on Mount Sinai and affirmed the covenant he made with the seed of Abraham, Isaac, and Jacob Israel. See Exodus 19:17-25, I'm paraphrasing, God came down on Mount Sinai and he gave Israel his laws, statutes, his judgments and he entered into a covenant with the nation Israel. See Exodus 34: 27, 28, The Lord said unto Moses, write thou these words for after the tenor of these words, I have made a covenant with thee and with Israel. Verse 28 and he was there with the Lord forty days and forty nights, he did neither eat bread nor drink water and he wrote upon the tables the words of the covenant, the Ten Commandments! What did this God look like that descended upon Mount Sinai? Let's see if the bible can answer this; run with me to Revelation the 1st chapter and verses 12,13,14 and 15. Verse14, his head and his hairs were white like **wool (nappy hair-afro)** as white as snow and **his eyes were as a flame of fire** (not blue eyed) verse 15 and **his feet like unto fine brass as if they burned in a furnace** (not white feet), this is the God that showed up on Mount Sinai. What color did the ancient Israelites paint their God?

IMAGE OF CHRIST, COPTIC MUSEUM, CAIRO EGYPT

As you can see the Coptic's of Cairo Egypt painted the Christ according to the Bibles description of him but I have other witnesses than this. See the image on the next page.

Mavriótissa Monastery Narthex (northern Greece) circa 1,200 A.D. | The Last Judgement - close-up

THE JUDGEMENT-MAVRIOTISSA MONASTRY GREECE

IMAGE DATED TO 1200 A.D

In every scene the ancients painted the Jesus of the Bible black but what about the Pope? He proclaims himself to be God's representative on Earth doesn't he? The word in Rome is the guy is infallible, all seeing and all knowing; then he should know what Jesus/YHSW looks like. So then…let's see what God he worships. Now I don't want you to go and get all teary eyed about what you are about to see on the next couple of pages but it is written," **You shall know the truth and the truth shall set you free." I am about to set a whole lot of you mentally free today.**

ONE OF THE SECRETS OF THE EUROPEANS

POPE JOHN PAUL PRAYS TO BLACK JESUS
1992 READERS DIGEST PAGE-222

POPE BENEDICT PRAYS TO BLACK JESUS

Pope John Paul the 2nd went to visit Angola in 1992 and bowed before the image of black Jesus. Would he have done this if Jesus was not black! These Popes are supposed to be the wisest men on Earth right? The Popes are giving the Churches a sign and what is that? In a subtle way they are telling the Churches that Jesus and the Jews are black....**they know**! Do you think that these are the only images of a black Jesus? Practically all of Europe worships a black Jesus and Mary. See images below.

133

JESUS IN FRANCE   JESUS IN BRAZIL   JESUS IN SPAIN

JESUS AND MARY MEYMAC FRANCE

JESUS WITH MARY　　　　　　JESUS WITH MARY-RUSSIA
BENEDICTINE ABBEY-SPAIN

All over the world the nations and the Papacy recognize a black Christ but in one place, the minds of the black man in America. This people have been so thoroughly Willie Lynched by the churches and the educational institutions in the United States that they cannot believe the truth. When you open up the book of Revelation (Revelation1:9-12) and show the black man that Jesus has nappy hair and burnt feet….he tells you it doesn't matter what color Jesus is. This brain washed black man doesn't understand that if he doesn't know what his God looks like he will fall for the anti-Christ when he appears…..**it does make a difference.**

SIEGE OF LACHISH ASSYRIA   CAN BE FOUND BRITISH &
2 KINGS 18:14   FRENCH MUSEUM

THIS TABLET READS THE AMO OR THE PEOPLE OF AM'

When the black man can imagine that his God looks like him then the reconstruction of his mind can begin....this is the first step…when he acknowledges what the World already knows; that the people of AMO or the people of God, looked just like their God, oh my… this is a surprise isn't it? The God of Israel looks just like his people. All nations paint images of their God to look like them. The only people on earth that I am acutely aware of that worships a God that doesn't look like them is this so called Negro in America! I would like to pose a question to you, what did Adam look like? The book of Genesis **(Genesis 1:26 & 27)** said," let us make man in our image and in our likeness, **so God made man in his own image** and likeness." So what did God look like? The book of Revelation has the answer, see Revelation **(Revelation1:9-15)** the son of man had **hair like lamb's wool (nappy)** and feet that looked as if they were burned in a furnace. **Adam looked like the son of man-Jesus**, he had an **afro** and was **a black man**…he looked like his father…..Jesus!

THESE CURSES SHALL BE FOR A SIGN

After he had given the fathers his covenant he told the fathers that if they walked in the sins of the nations around them that they would be cursed and that these curses would be on Israel for a sign and wonder. Let's examine these curse signs and you tell me who they are pointing toward. Open your King James Bible to Deuteronomy **(Deuteronomy 28:14-68)**, verse 14" and thou shall not go aside from any of the words which I command thee this day to the right hand or to the left to go after other gods to serve them. Verse 15 but it shall come to pass if thou wilt not hearken unto the voice of the lord thy God to observe to do all his commandments and his statutes which I command thee this day that all these curses shall come upon thee and overtake thee: verse 16 **cursed shall thou be in the city and cursed shall thou be in the field. The so called Negro was cursed when he toiled the fields for free in the south and he was cursed under sharecropping. Then under the great migration from 1910-1930 and 1940-1970 he moved north to the cities and became a city dweller, but the curse followed him north. He couldn't find a job and he couldn't support his family,** so he was cursed in the field and cursed in the city. **Deuteronomy 28th Chapter continued;** Verse 28 the Lord shall smite thee with madness and blindness (who is blinder than the black man?) and astonishment of heart, verse 29 and thou shall grope at noonday as the blind gropes in darkness and thou shall not prosper in thy ways and thou shall be only oppressed and spoiled evermore and no man shall save thee. This 29th verse states that you will be oppressed and spoiled. **Who is more oppressed than the Negro**? Who is spoiled more than the Negro? I don't care what nations you find us in... we are oppressed. Deuteronomy 28th Chapter continued; Verse 37 and thou shall become an astonishment, a proverb, and a byword among all nations where the Lord shall lead thee. What do you think the thought is that comes to other ethnic groups minds when they see how the Negro lives and conducts himself? You know what a byword is? Example; **coon, blackie, jungle bunny, monkey, sambo, stepping fetching**, and let us not forget the N word.

28TH CHAPTER OF DEUTERONOMY CONTINUED:

Verse 43, the stranger that is within thee shall get up above you very high and thou shall come down very low. Think for a moment who owns the businesses in the black community? **The Asians sell our women their hair, the Spanish sell us our produce, the Arabs sell us our liquor and the Indians sell us our gasoline**. All of the vendors that come to our neighborhood and sell to us look like somebody else. The money that they make in our neighborhood they take back and deposit in their banks. This is what the scripture means when it says the stranger shall get very high and you shall be low. **Deuteronomy Chapter 28 continued;** Verse 44, he shall lend to thee and thou shall not lend to him he shall be the head and thou shall be the tail. This can't be pointing to the European Jew because he is the banker of this generation and he does all of the lending. The so called Negro does all the borrowing. Verse 46 and they (curses) shall be upon thee for a sign and for a wonder and upon thy seed forever. You see when you saw all of these signs you were supposed to wake up to consciousness, to self to say hey, that looks like me! You never read this because your Minister told you that you are a New Testament Christian, so you never examined the writings of the prophets. See Isaiah 42: 22, this is a people robbed and spoiled they are all of them snared in holes and **they are hid in prison houses**. Half of the inmates in this country are black but the Negro only makes up twelve percent of the population. Isaiah 42: verse 24, who gave Jacob for a spoil and Israel to the robbers did not the Lord he against whom we have sinned? For they would not walk in his ways neither were they obedient unto his law! Verse 25, **therefore he hath poured upon him the fury of his anger and the strength** of battle and it hath set him on fire round about yet he knew not and it burned him **yet he laid it not to heart. This is family business between us and our God** and the strange thing is the Lord said thru the prophet Isaiah," **It never came to your mind (heart) that all of the things that befell you Mr. Negro... was from my hand.** This quarrel was and is a family dispute between the God of Israel and his people...**it's just playing out in front of the global community.** What he did to us was a warning to the rest of the world; God is not a respecter of persons, all men are judged the same. See Leviticus **(Leviticus 26: 15- 46)** verse 21, if you walk contrary unto me and will not hearken unto me I will bring seven times more plagues upon you according to your sin. Verse 23 and if you will not be reformed by me by these things but will walk contrary unto me verse 24 then will I also walk contrary unto you and will punish you yet seven times for your sins verse 25 and **I will send a sword upon you that shall avenge <u>the quarrel of my covenant.</u>** This is what I have been saying all along; **God has a running quarrel (argument) with the so-called Negro.** Ladies and gentlemen this is why the so called Negro is in the economic, social, and mental condition that he finds himself in, no matter where you find him. This is the reason that we were spread out among all the nations on earth because of this family dispute between us and our God! What is God's bone of contention with the black Hebrew Israelite? We refuse to keep his commandments and to walk in his statues; we worship the gods of the nations around about us! And so we were delivered into the hands of our enemies. See Leviticus **(Leviticus 26: verse 17)** verse 17 and I will set my face against you and ....**they that hate you shall reign over you** and you shall flee when none pursues you, verse 33 and **I will scatter you among the heathen. A heathen and a barbarian is the same thing.** The Government sponsored history books state," **the barbarians** overran the Western leg of the Roman Empire." Who are they talking about? They are talking about the Angles and the Saxons but these people have passed off the World scene. Did these barbarians leave a seed behind? Let Benjamin Franklin answer this question for you.

BENJAMIN FRANKLIN
AMERICA AS A LAND OF OPPORTUNITY 1751

"Which leads me to add one Remark; that **the Number of purely white People in the World is proportionally very small. The Saxons only excepted, who with the English, make the principal Body of White People on the Face of the Earth**. I could wish their Numbers were increased."

The seed of the Barbarians are the Anglo Saxons and the English? The seed of the barbarians became the current European Nations; America, France, Spain, Portugal, Italy, Rome, Western Europe, Eastern Europe, parts of Asia, Arabia and the Middle East. The seed of the barbarian can be found all over the Earth!

Why do the Europeans hate the so-called Negro? Is it because we made them materially rich and continue to do so? I doubt it....I think it has something to do with real history and how he was treated by black people. I know how the current European(**Leper**) was treated, no one wanted him around. The Great Wall of China (**221 B.C**)was built to keep the current European out. Hadrian's Wall **(122 A.D)** in England was built to keep the barbarian out. read the article on the next page written by Professor Boyd Dawkins concerning the invasion of the barbarians into England and Britain.....you will be amazed!

PROFESSOR BOYD DAWKINS, 1837-1929
OUR EARLIEST ANCESTORS, PAGE 96 & 97

In the year A.D 449 certain Englishmen, for they were Englishmen before our England had received its name, **came over here from the** North of Germany **and from** the **Southern shores of the Baltic Sea.** Based on this testimony and the testimony of Benjamin Franklin one has to conclude that the European American is not descended from the Caucus Mountains because the Caucuses run thru Russia! See map on next page.

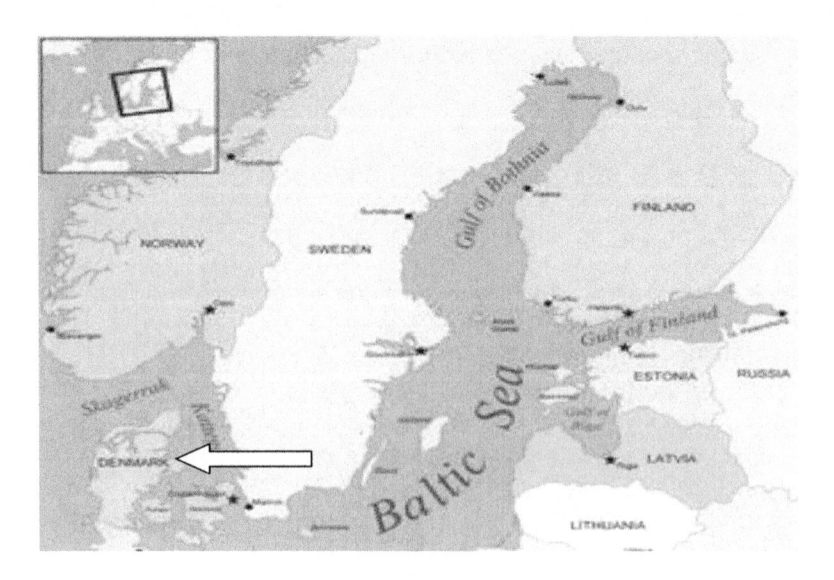

GOOGLE MAPS

I followed Professor Boyd Dawkins lead and that of Benjamin Franklin and true enough, the Angle and Saxons came from North of Germany and the Southern shores of the Baltic Sea.

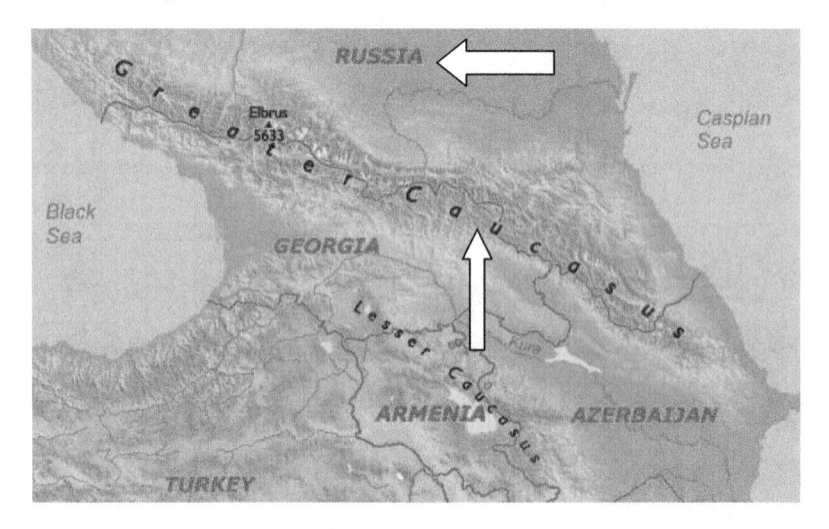

GOOGLE MAPS

As you can see....the Caucus Mountains are near Russia not Germany....what is going on?

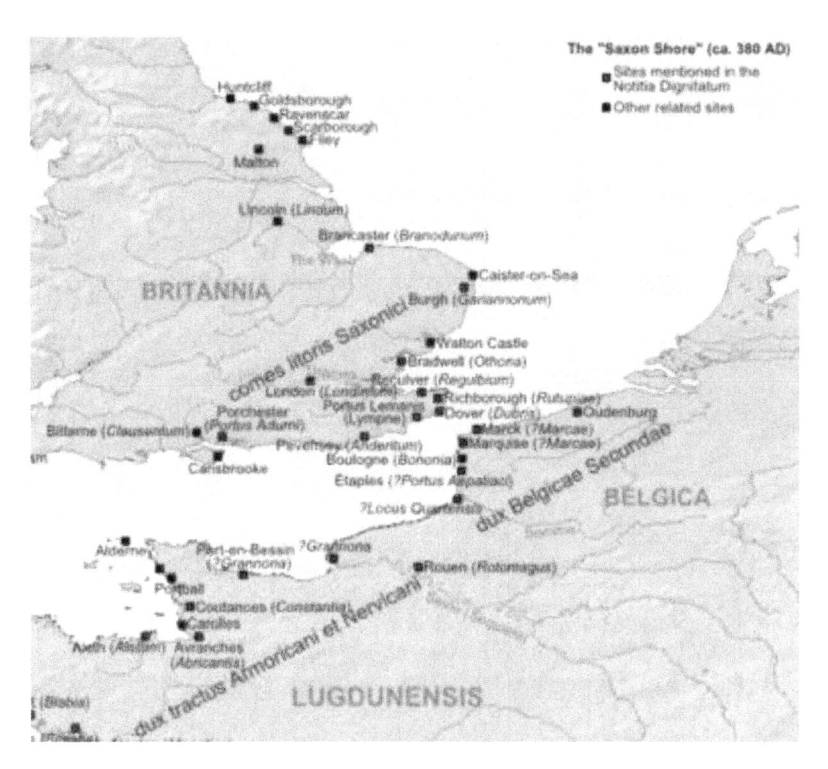

GOOGLE MAPS

PROFESSOR BOYD DAWKINS CONTINUED

"After a long war of conquest and a series of battles they gradually pushed away west that population which had been in possession of this country before it was England....**during that time it was known as Britain.**"

The year that Professor Dawkins references **(449 A.D)** is identical to the year that the Government sponsored history books give (450 A.D) for the invasion and destruction of the Western leg of the Roman Empire....**BY THE BARBARIANS!**

PROFESSOR BOYD DAWKINS CONTINUED

"The people whom these barbarians displaced called themselves Roman citizens."These are the black Brits and Scots....I shall prove that later in this book. Notice what the Professor says next.

PROFESSOR BOYD DAWKINS CONTINUED

"**Our fathers (barbarians) were not men of peace, they were men of war and they burned and destroyed everything that was Roman**, everything that **was British**, everything that **was termed Welsh, for we owe the term Welsh to them** and they destroyed that civilization by fire and sword. **The Welsh or ancient Britain was a short dark/black man.**" By the year <u>**A.D 607 our fathers had pushed the black British as far as Chester, Scotland, Wales, Cumberland, Westmoreland, Cornwall and Devon.**</u>

The **black Roman Britain's fought off the white barbarians for 158 years**....that's a long time to be fighting...whew!! The Roman historian Tacitus said," <u>**they (Saxons & Angle) never lived in cities but they lived in underground caves;**</u> **they had red hair and blue eyes.**"

Benjamin Franklin and Professor Boyd Dawkins knew their history ...it appears that this modern historian doesn't.

BENJAMIN FRANKLIN'S ESSAY CONTINUED
AMERICA AS A LAND OF OPPORTUNITY 1751

"Which leads me to add one Remark: That **the Number of purely white People in the World is proportionally very small. <u>The Saxons who with the English (Angle) make the principal Body of White People on the Face of the Earth.</u>** I could wish their Numbers were increased.

Benjamin Franklin and Professor Boyd Dawkins testimony concerning the Europeans in America is the truth!

FURTHER PROOF
DR. LAIN MATTHIESON-GENETICIST AT HARVARD UNIVERSITY

"Ancient D.N.A makes it possible to examine populations as they were before and after adaptation. Dark skinned, **black people arrived in Europe 40,000 years ago and retained their black skin far longer than originally thought.**"

PROOF CONTINUED
PALLAB GHOSH, SCIENCE CORRESPONDENT, BBC NEWS
NOVEMBER 23, 2015

"The researcher's plan to analyze more of the 20,000 human remains stored at the Museum of London. According to Caroline

McDonald, who is a senior curator at the museum, **"London was a cosmopolitan city from the moment it was created** following the Roman invasion 2000 years ago."**THIS IS A LIE!**

I could take this statement from this geneticist and gloat but there is one problem with her research. Pallab Ghosh said that the city of London was a cosmopolitan city 2000 years ago....that is mathematically impossible.

ARTICLE WRITTEN	2015	A.D
2000 YEARS AGO	-2000	
	15	A.D

PROFESSOR BOYD	449 A.D	
DAWKINS DATE FOR		
THE ARRIVAL OF		
THE BARBARIANS	449	A.D

THE CITY OF LONDON WAS FOUNDED BY THE BLACK BRITAINS 434 YEARS BEFORE THE BARBARIANS ARRIVED.

The geneticist said that the barbarians arrived in Britain in 15 A.D but Professor Boyd Dawkins said the actual date for their arrival was 434 years later **(449 B.C)**. What does this mean? **This means that the black Britain's were the original founders of London**.... the barbarians arrived 434 years after its founding! This is the reason why the Europeans in the South conducted themselves like barbarians during the North Atlantic Slave trade...because they were. This modern European just became civilized...recently!

THE LYNCHING OF UNARMED MEN WOMEN AND CHILDREN

CURSED IS HE THAT HANGS ON A TREE

DEUTERONOMY 21:22 & 23

This was the time that the Lord talked about when he said your life would hang in doubt. The **Tuskegee Institute recorded 3,446 lynching's** in the south between the years 1882 and 1968. Nearly 200 lynching bills were introduced into Congress but only 3 passed the House, seven Presidents between 1890 and 1952 petitioned Congress to pass a federal law. It couldn't get past the Senate. This was the mental condition of the Europeans in America and this is what our fathers had to deal with. Think about it after 246 years of free labor the Negro should have been loved by these Southern European's but that would not be the case. I guess they must have missed the free labor, raping, killing, stealing and taking other nations lands. Do the Europeans hate the black man because the curse from the Garden of Eden has overtaken him? Genesis **(Genesis 3:19)** verse 19, **in the sweat of thy face shall you eat bread, till you return unto the ground;** for out of it were you taken, for dust you are and dust you shall return. No man is exempt from this decree!

JIM CROW LAWS 1876-1965

These laws provided for the segregation of public places, bathrooms, restaurants, public schools, drinking fountains and the Military! While writing this book I have begun to realize that the European church in America failed God, for if this institution had stood on the side of righteousness the criminal institution of slavery could never have gained a footing on American soil. I must note the fact that under segregation the Negro owned his own businesses; the Negro professional baseball league, Black Wall Street, and he received an education from those who loved him! He was taught to love himself, when people love you they point out the error of your ways, they tell you what not to do… to succeed in life. This was the type of mentoring and tutoring that we received from the segregated black schools that we ran. The black child was taught the truth about his former glory.

CURSED IN THE FIELD AND CURSED IN THE CITY

DEUTERONOMY 28:16

This is what awaited the black man when he left the cotton fields and went into the city!

No matter where Israel went in this country **the quarrel of the covenant** followed him, the curses that would be on him for a sign followed him from the country to the city. **God says he was slightly displeased but the heathen helped further the affliction,** meaning they went too far! At about this time the white man in America had just about rolled back the clock on any gains this Negro had achieved since 1865 and he had his foot so far up the Negros' behind that he probably thought he had grown another leg. But again the God of Israel heard the moaning and groaning of his people Israel in America and he raised us up saviors. This section here is for all of you zealots and fanatics in America; some of you think that if a brother or sister has not come into the knowledge of self that he is to be shown disdain and contempt. That brother or sister is still the inheritance of the Lord and don't you forget it. In the process of time the Lord will open up his or her eyes just like he did yours and mine. Remember that you once also were blind and now you see. This was not by any act of your own but by the mercy of a loving God.

CHAPTER 9   IF IT BE A SON KILLHIM

Read the book of Nehemiah **(Nehemiah 9:26& 27)** verse 26, nevertheless they were disobedient and rebelled against thee and cast thy law behind their backs and slew thy prophets which testified against them to turn them to thee and they wrought great provocations. Verse 27, therefore thou delivered them into the hands of their enemies who vexed them and **in the time of their trouble when they cried unto thee thou heard them from heaven** and according to thy manifold mercies **thou gave them saviors** who saved them out of the hand of their enemies! Once again the living God intervened on our behalf when he sent us Martin Luther King. I must put this in here because the Lord is not limited in his power, he can deliver with a blind man or a seeing man, a Hebrew or a Muslim, a Christian or a Buddhist. The Lord can use a wicked man or a righteous man, there really is no searching out his ways but the fact is.... he can deliver like no other. If a man is drowning will he care if the object that saves him is a tree vine or a floating log? Will he care if his deliverance came by way of a Jew or a Muslim, I say nay! His only saying will be thank God! I would like to examine two saviors of the Negro race Martin Luther King and Malcolm X.

RARE IMAGE OF MARTIN AND MALCOM X

MARTIN L. KING WITH MALCOM-X
CBS NEWS, GETTY IMAGES, GOOGLE

The most high brought Martin Luther King along at a time when the heads of all the black men in America stooped for shame. History talks about the march on Washington, Europeans hadn't seen that many Hebrews in one place in their entire life. Martin will be remembered for the Rosa Parks Montgomery bus incident in 1955, where this mother in Israel uttered those famous words that echoed around the globe," **NO!** I refuse to get up out of my seat and move to the back of the bus! Martin will be remembered for the garbage strikes, the Birmingham protests and the Nobel Peace Prize. I think all of these accomplishments, **though great**, were pale in comparison for what he really did; **Martin helped to reconstruct the mental psyche of the Black man in America!**

Martin showed the brothers and sisters (we) together can turn the world upside down and they did! A very interesting fact about Martin Luther King was that he and Malcolm had come to an understanding of working together for the sake of the Negro nation. In fact few people are aware that Martin Luther King had started to form his own party to run for the Presidency of the United States. In 1967 William F. Pepper suggested to King that he should challenge Lyndon B. Johnson for the Democratic Party nomination but King refused. Martin Luther King was going to form his own party! The National Conference for New Politics, this was the platform he would use for a presidential run with Dr. Benjamin Spock as his Vice President. It appears that Martin and Malcolm decided that the way to get justice was to use the vote to their advantage....run for presidency and manage the country. I think that Martin and Malcolm underestimated the greed of the international bank of gangsters, **sorry I meant bankers**. This may have been what excited his enemies to assassinate him.

**FUNERAL PROCESSION OF MARTIN L. KING
ATLANTA JOURNAL 1968**

Exodus (**Exodus 1:15& 16**) verse 15, the king of Egypt spoke to the Hebrew midwives, of which the name of the one was Shiph-rah and the name of the other Pu'ah verse 16 and he said," when you do the office of a midwife to the Hebrew women and see them upon the stools, **if it be a son then you shall kill him** but if it be a daughter... she shall live!

This was the attitude of Pharaohs generation; it was the attitude of the Europeans in Martin Luther King's generation and this is attitude of this current European American generation. Take notice, the racist Europeans **didn't kill Coretta King** did they? They didn't kill Malcolm's wife either and do you know why? Because the commandment is still the same, let the black woman live, but kill the black men. What happened to Martin was genocide. Let's examine the United Nation definition of genocide.

Genocide

Article II: In the present Convention, genocide means any of the following acts committed with intent to destroy, in whole or in part, a national, ethnical, racial or religious group, as such:

A-KILLING MEMBERS OF THE GROUP

B-CAUSING SERIOUS BODILY OR MENTAL HARM TO MEMBERS OF THE GROUP

C-DELIBERATELY INFLICTING ON THE GROUP CONDITIONS OF LIFE, CALCULATED TO BRING ABOUT ITS PHYSICAL DESTRUCTION IN WHOLE OR IN PART.

D-IMPOSING MEASURES INTENDED TO PREVENT BIRTHS WITHIN THE GROUP

E-FORCIBLY TRANSFERRING CHILDREN OF THE GROUP TO ANOTHER GROUP

Article III: The following acts shall be punishable:

GENOCIDE;

A-CONSPIRACY TO COMMIT GENOCIDE

B-ATTEMPT TO COMMIT GENOCIDE

C-COMPLICITY IN GENOCIDE

D-DIRECT AND PUBLIC INCITEMENT TO COMMIT GENOCIDE

Looking backwards from our present vantage point, we can clearly see that what happened to Martin L. King is defined as Genocide under the U.N Charter. What about the brothers who have been murdered by racist white cops, electrocuted legally on the streets of this country **(taser)** or who have died on death row for crimes they did not commit? Is this too not genocide? What about the savage organization in all the poor Negro communities called Planned Parenthood? Let's dive into statistics for a moment; **550,000 black babies** are aborted by Planned Parenthood each year in the United States. That means fifteen million black babies have been murdered in the last thirty years. **Is this not imposing measures to prevent births in a group, the black community?** Rest in peace elder King we will see you in the resurrection and you will indeed wear the crown of a King, peace!

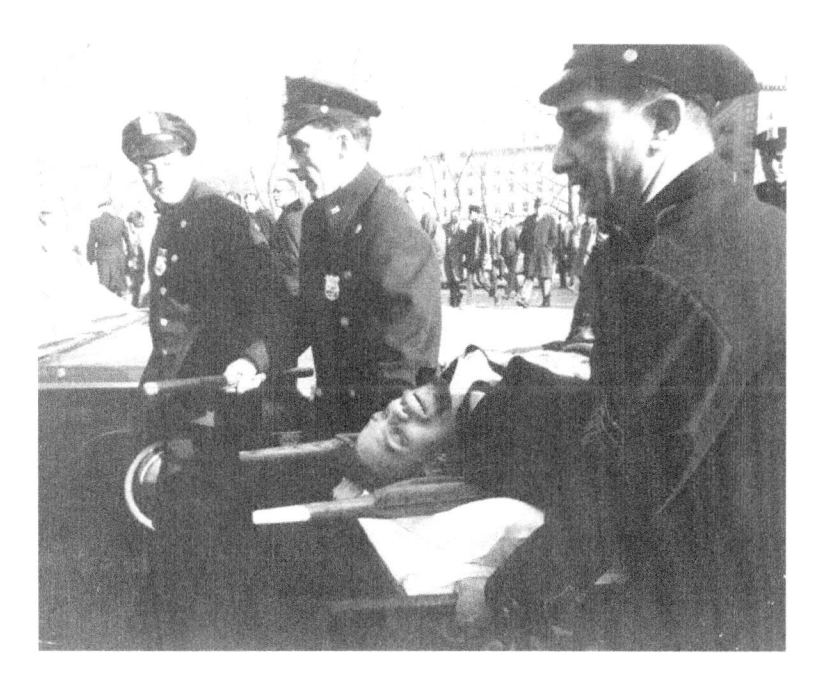

MALCOLM X BODY BEING CARRIED BY POLICE
NEWYORK TIMES 1965

Any student of so called African American history knows the story of Malcolm little or Malcolm X, he started life as a street hustler. He eventually went to prison where he learned how to read and write. He joined the Nation of Islam and became an activist, that's right; he fought for the real freedom of the Hebrew Israelite in America. Malcolm represented the military side of our conflict in America. He was intelligent and articulate but most of all the man was fearless. Malcolm's focus was **nationhood** for the Negro because this man understood from the historical record that we are the seed of the empire. I used to get a rush about our fathers in Africa building 54 nations but if you add the Western Sahara and Somaliland that would make 56. I read the account of the **Ashanti Empire and** I began to understand what this seed is really capable of. The European historians in this captivity know that what I write is free of lies. Malcolm's **wife and daughter went unharmed** because it is written, **"if it's a daughter you shall save it alive."** The commandment, if it be a son kill him, is not relegated to just the black man. What I've noticed throughout history is that any white man that will try to help this captive Negro will also be killed. Here are a few examples; **President Lincoln, John F. Kennedy, John Brown and Robert Kennedy.** Two Governors in the state of Illinois have been incarcerated for helping black people; Governor Thompson and Governor Blagojevich. Governor Thompson did away with the death penalty; he saw the statistics of the innocent black men dying on death row for crimes they did not commit. The State of Illinois had this Governor incarcerated. Rest in peace **General Malcolm**...your sacrifice is real and the guys understand what you did....your heart was big as a lion...you will receive a crown in the resurrection.

ULTERIOR MOTIVE FOR KILLING BLACK MEN

When Nations conquer one another in war they generally kill all the males and take the women as wives or concubines. This gruesome ideology goes back 6000 years and it appears that this is one of the hidden agendas in the United States; kill off the black man and take the black woman as a wife or concubine. The propaganda tool that is being used to promote this idea is Hollywood. You can't turn your television on anymore and not see the black woman with her black child and a European husband! Think about this for one moment, the Government has a commercial where they are recruiting young black males into the military....they have the black son with his black mother and the black father is left out of the commercial altogether. The propaganda tool shows the same commercial but this time the advertisement shows a European son talking to his European father about enlisting in the army...do you see the difference. The black man is subliminally omitted from the black son's life. We have to resist the narrative just like our fathers resisted the narrative, that they were slaves.

MEDGAR EDGARS 1925-1963

CIVIL RIGHTS ACTIVIST – GOOGLE, WIKEPEDIA

There is no way that I could leave out this brother from Alcorn State who gave his life in registering black voters in the South. Medgar Edgars was an N.A.A.C.P activist who gave his life for his people. A white KKK member, **Byron De La Beckwith**, who murdered Medgar in 1963 was acquitted by two all white juries in the State of Mississippi. This murderer was not convicted until 30 years later! The edict of Pharaoh still held sway, if it be a son kill him but let the woman live. Medgar Edgars' wife and children were spared. Rest in peace field general....you also shall receive a crown in the resurrection.

CHAPTER 10   THE UNTHINKABLE

**JOSEPH-GOVERNOR OF EGYPT-1917 B.C
CAIRO MUSEUM-EGYPT-3900 YR OLD IMAGE**

The Lord says that if he didn't intervene then the enemy would vaunt himself and say the Lord has not done this. The enemy would have said," I did this to them." See Deuteronomy 32:26, & 27 verse 26, I said, **I would scatter them into corners**, I would make **the remembrance of them to cease from among men** verse 27, were it not that I feared the wrath of **the enemy**, lest their adversaries should **behave themselves strangely**, and lest **they should say our hand is high and the Lord has not done all of this!** As a result of the quarrel of the covenant the so called Negro finds himself in the hands of those that hate him, (Europeans) it was necessary for the Lord to scatter the black

Israelite into all the nations under the sun. History records that we were the greatest fighting men that the world had ever seen; the nations feared the black man. See Deuteronomy 32:30 verse 30, how should **one chase a thousand and two put ten thousand to flight**; this is one of the reasons I knew that the hand of the Lord was against us. There is no way that any nation on Earth could defeat the black man in battle or control him unless our God had permitted it! **History teaches us that in our times of hardship the Lord raises up one of the brothers to sit on the throne of our enemies;** he did it when Joseph and the elders were in Egypt. The most high raised Joseph out of prison and made him ruler next to Pharaoh. See Genesis 41:38 & 39 verse 38, Pharaoh said unto his servants, can we find such a one as this is, a man in whom the spirit of God is? Verse 40, you shall be over my house and according unto thy word shall all my people be ruled only in the throne will I be greater than you. This is an image of Joseph that was found on a coin in the land of Egypt, as you can see he is a black Hebrew Israelite, and according to the article the back of the coin had images of wheat and corn and named Joseph Viceroy of Egypt. **If you take this image of Joseph and match it with the pictures that came out of the tomb of Beni Hassan** you will have a perfect match; Joseph looks like the rest of the brothers and sisters whose images were on the wall of the tomb.

TIME LINE FOR JOSEPH
AND THE NAME OF THE PHARAOHS THAT PROMOTED HIM

CREATION OF ADAM	4142	B.C
1656 YRS PASSED TO THE FLOOD	-1656	YRS
	2486	B.C
	-292	YRS
BIRTH OF ABRAHAM	2194	B.C
	-100	YRS
BIRTH OF ISAAC	2094	
	-60	YRS
BIRTH OF JACOB	2034	B.C
	-91	YRS
BIRTH OF JOSEPH	1943	B.C
	-17	
JOSEPH SOLD INTO EGYPT-17 YEARS OLD	1926	B.C
	-13	
JOSEPH IS 30 YEARS OLD GOVERNOR OF ALL EGYPT	1913	B.C

PHARAOH AMENHETET 1925 B.C - 1825 B.C
12TH DYNASTY OF EGYPT
EGYPTIAN MUSEUM, CAIRO EGYPT

This is the Pharaoh that promoted Joseph to be Governor over all the land of Egypt and I will prove it. The secret to this Biblical neglect by the Bible translators is in Pharaoh Amenhetet's son's name. See the Tablet below.

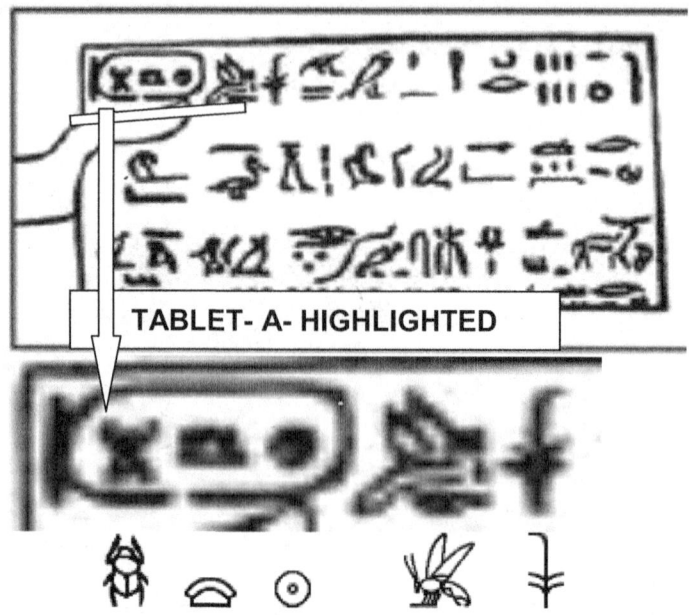

TABLET FOUND IN THE TOMB OF BENI-HASAN-EGYPT

TABLET- A- HIGHLIGHTED

This tablet was taken from the tomb of Beni Hasan in Egypt and it reads," the Hebrews (Hyskos) entered Egypt in the 6th year reign of Khakheperre (Senusret 2). Before a Pharaoh was born he was given a prenomen name and a nomen. **Senusret2 prenomen name was Khakhepere and that is the name that appears on this tablet.** Khakheperres' 6th year would have been in the year

166

1891 B.C. and this means Joseph would have been promoted by Amenhetet 2. I proved this with my timeline but this tablet is an official document which validates my research. I have one more piece of evidence which cannot be ignored, there is a canal in Egypt that has Josephs name on it and guess what? It has been dated to the 12th dynasty of Egypt.

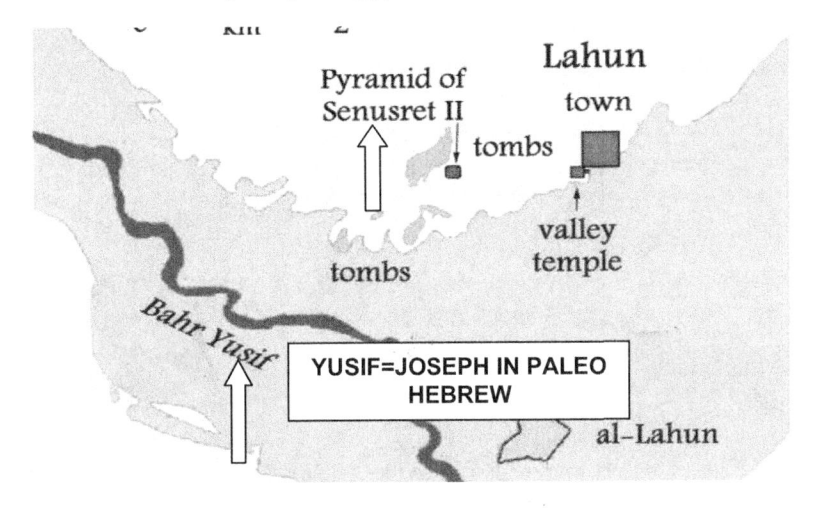

Map showing Pyramid of Senusret II, Lahun town, tombs, valley temple, Bahr Yusif canal, and al-Lahun. Label: YUSIF=JOSEPH IN PALEO HEBREW

GOOGLE MAPS

Khakheperre Senusret II was the fourth pharaoh of the Twelfth Dynasty of Egypt. He ruled from 1897 BC to 1878 BC. His pyramid was constructed at El-Lahun. Senusret II took a great deal of interest in the Faiyum oasis region and began work on an extensive irrigation system. This canal **(Bahr Yusif)** was named after Joseph and was built during the 12th dynasty of Egypt...Joseph's era. If you want to read all of my research on this matter sees the Negro Question Part 5, Joseph and the 12th Dynasty of Egypt. Yusif is Yosaph in Hebrew or Joseph in English.

WHEN FOUR BLACK MEN RULED THE WHOLE WORLD TOGETHER!

ST. MARKS BASILICA, VENICE ITALY
AND CATHOLIC ENCYCLOPEDIA

The Portrait of the Four Tetrarchs depicts the four rulers in charge of the entire Empire, instituted by **Emperor Diocletian. The Caesar he chose was Galerius**, and they ruled over the Eastern half of the Empire, while the Western half was ruled by **Augustus Maximian and Caesar Constantinius Chlorus,** father of Constantine the Great. You can find this image in the Catholic Encyclopedia. What did the black Britain's call themselves? They called themselves Roman citizens.

BLACK ROMAN EMPEROR SERVERUS CAESAR

193A.D-211A.D

Septimius Serverus was a North African Libyan who ruled the Holy Roman Empire around193 A.D. Ham was the son of Noah and the father of the Libyans. With this basic Biblical information we should have been able to deduce **(figure out)** that Severus was a black man! The rulership of the World by black people is not an anomaly (freak happening) it is the norm. The so-called Negro (Hebrew) gave the World the basis for nation building when we gave them the laws and statutes of the creator. Without these basic laws **(Ten Commandments)** the entire planet would be lawless!

BLACK CAESAR-SEVERUS SEPTIMUS

THE SEVERAN TONDO 199 B.C

ANTIKENSAMMLUNG, BERLIN

You have to admit giving this chapter the title the unthinkable is appropriate isn't it? Who would have ever dreamed in a million years that the so-called Negro sat on the throne of some of the greatest Empires the World had ever seen….think about it!

JESSE JACKSON 1941-STILL ALIVE!

I witnessed the running for the presidency of the United States by Jesse Jackson in 1984….. a black man. At that time, based on what had been taught to me by my European professors and my ignorant black professors I thought that these events were the first of its kind. You can't kick against Jesse, his record in the human rights arena speaks for itself. In 1983 he cabled Assad **(Dictator of Syria)** directly to plead for the release of downed pilot Robert Goodman Jr. When Assad failed to respond, Jackson flew to Damascus and worked his way through a tangle of lower-level Syrian bureaucrats before securing a meeting with the Syrian leader. The success of that mission jump started Jackson's 1984 Presidential campaign. He had hostages released in Cuba, Iraq, and Yugoslavia. He created Operation Bread Basket and initiated boycotts. I failed to mention he was with Martin Luther King during the civil rights movement. He has made mistakes along the way **(who hasn't)** he still deserves a place in the Negro Hall of Fame. Jesse would never wear the crown in America....it was reserved for one Barack Obama.

U.S PRESIDENT, BARACK OBAMA

JANUARY 2009-JANUARY 2017

It's interesting to note how these Europeans have portrayed the election of Barak Obama in the United States as some sort of phenomenon. These historians would have you to believe that this was the first time in human history that a black man ruled over a European nation, let alone a European empire. This is the reason it is important that these Negro historians who have been taught a curriculum at these European institutions' and the racist historians do some real research. It is time to tell the truth, not just too black people but to the whole World. So far the legacy of Barrack Obama is still being written but I will go on record to say that to hold the title of the most powerful man in the world and to be treated the way he has by this racist white media is mind boggling.

CHAPTER 11   THE MORNING TRAIN

I would like to put a question to you, who told the Negro that his sojourning in the land of the Indians would last forever? The God of Israel set a time limit on the outcasts of Israel and **believe it or not our sojourning in North America, is tied into the time that God has set for the Europeans to rule the earth**. These are ancient things that I am about to speak about, the Lord set the bounds of human civilization in the writings of the Prophet Moses. In the book of Leviticus **(Leviticus 23: 3)** verse 3, six days shall work be done but the seventh day is the Sabbath of rest, a holy convocation, ye shall do no work therein it is the Sabbath of the Lord in all your dwellings. **This is the first clue**, the Lord told Moses that **this man has 6 days to work**; is God talking about mans days or what? We'll have to travel back to the very beginning and ear hustle on a conversation that God is having with Adam about the concept of a day. See Genesis (Genesis 2:16 & 17) verse 16, the Lord God commanded the man saying of every tree of the garden thou may freely eat verse 17 but of the tree of the knowledge of good and evil thou shall not eat of it,**for in the day that thou eat thereof thou shall surely die**. So now we have to see how many years make up one of Gods days. Lets' go to 2nd Pete r**(2nd Peter 3: 8)** verse 8, beloved be not ignorant of this one thing that **one day with the Lord is 1000 years and a thousand years one day**. King David wrote in the book of Psalm (Psalm

90:4) verse 4, **a thousand years in thy sight are but as yesterday** when it is past and as a watch in the night. All of this sounds good but can it be proven out? Let's see how long the old timers lived; let's see if any one of them lived to be 1000 years old.

ADAM -GENESIS 5:5 ALL THE DAYS OF ADAM WAS 930 AND HE DIED.

SETH- GENESIS 5:8 ALL THE DAYS OF SETH WAS 912 YEARS AND HE DIED.

ENOS- GENESIS 5:11 ALL THE DAYS OF ENOS WAS 905 YEARS AND HE DIED.

CAINAN- GENESIS 5:14 ALL THE DAYS OF CAINAN WAS 910 YEARS AND HE DIED.

MAHALALEEL- GENESIS 5:17 ALL THE DAYS OF MAHALALEEL WAS 895 YEARS AND HE DIED.

JARED-GENESIS 5:20 ALL THE DAYS OF JARED WAS 962 YEARS AND HE DIED.

METHUSALAH- GENESIS 5:27 ALL THE DAYS OF METHUSALAH WAS 969 YEARS AND HE DIED.

NOAH- GENESIS 9:29 ALL THE DAYS OF NOAH WAS 950 YEARS AND HE DIED.

ENOCH-GENEIS 5:24 ALL THE DAYS OF ENOCH WAS 365 AND GOD TOOK HIM!

As you can see, none of the old timers lived an entire day or one of God's days; which happen to be 1000 years. So when God gave man 6 days to work he really gave him 6000 years to govern the planet. The second part of this question is this.....how many years have elapsed of these 6000 years?

CALCULATION FOR 6000 YEARS

ADAM CREATED (REVISED AND ACCURATE DATE) 4142 B.C B.C

JESUS MURDERED ON CALVARY CROSS 29.5 A.D A.D

ONE DAY TO THE LORD IS 1000 YEARS AND 1000 YEARS IS ONE DAY!
FROM ADAM TO JESUS IS 4000 YEARS OR 4 DAYS .= 4 DAYS

JESUS/YSHW MURDERED ON CALVARY CROSS 29.5 A.D
FROM JESUS TO THIS GENERATION IS 2000 YEARS 2019 A.D

ONE DAY TO THE LORD IS 1000 YEARS AND 1000 YEARS IS ONE DAY!
FROM JESUS TO US IS 2000 YEARS= 2DAYS **2 DAYS**

6 DAYS OR 6000 YEARS HAVE ELAPSED SINCE ADAM CREATED= 6 DAYS

From the creation of Adam to the murder of Jesus/YSWH is exactly 4000 years; and from the murder of Jesus to our generation is exactly 2000 years. Are you smarter than a 5th grader? Four thousand plus two thousand equals 6000 years and since one day to the Lord is 1000 years it means 6 days have passed.....we are basically out of time! Is there any proof on the earth concerning this supposed hypothesis? Of course there is, for starters this man only has 6000 years of written history. The oldest writings on Earth have been unearthed in Mesopotamia and they are called cuneiform tablets.

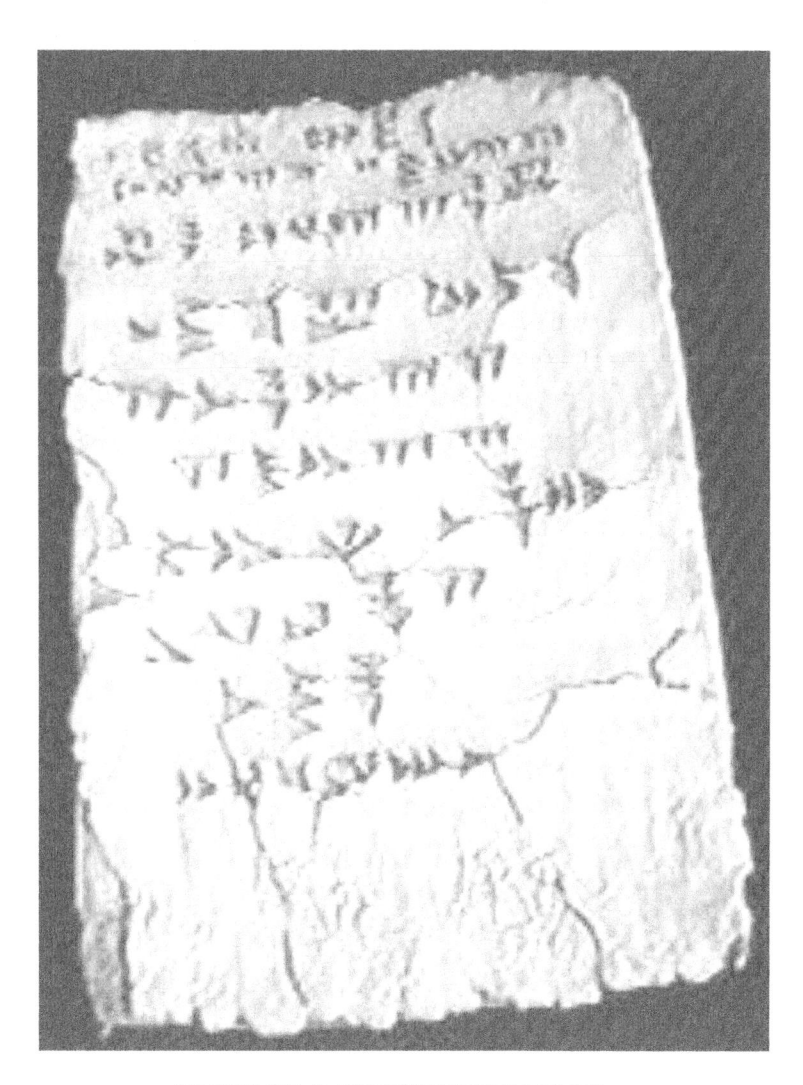

IMAGE OF A CUNEIFORM TABLET

BRITISH MUSEUM LONDON

The ancient Sumerians used wedged shape reeds from the Euphrates to write on these clay tablets and then they would let them dry in the sun. These clay tablets are still being translated.

GUDEA	SHULGI	SARGON
BRITISH MUSEUM	BRITISH MUSEUM	BRITISH MUSEUM

What these archaeologists are unearthing are the writings of the black headed ones of Shinar (Sumer); these are the black Mesopotamian's that the historians have written about so pointedly, stating that they are black but not the sons of Ham! The black men of Mesopotamia are the inventors of **math**, the **wheel**, the **sexagesamal system**, **astronomy**, **writing** and the **first medicine book** was found in Mesopotamia, In fact **the first known language is credited to these black men; <u>we were the first men on Earth to sound a vowel....to speak! The black man was the first to walk and the first to read!</u> We are the first of our kind....man!** This may be the reason the European historians have been lying all these years, saying that Africa is the cradle of civilization, when in fact Mesopotamia is the cradle of civilization. They did not want you to know that Adam, Seth, Cainan, Enos, Mahalaeel, Methusalah, Enoch, Lamech, Jared and Noah were all black Mesopotamian men! In the book of Genesis **(Genesis 2:14)** God said that he put Adam and Eve near the Tigris and Euphrates river.

Ladies and gentleman the Tigris and Euphrates runs thru Mesopotamia. The archaeologists say the oldest bones were found in Africa. **I have no problem with that, people go for walks all the time, the person started his walk in Mesopotamian and walked over into Africa.** Let God be true and every man a liar. The Sumerians used a reed (like a drinking straw) to draw web shaped images in clay and then they would either bake the clay or allow them to dry in the sun. **You have been taught all of your life that Egypt was the oldest civilization, and this is a lie.** The oldest civilization on earth was **Adam's civilization** and it was located in **Mesopotamia, the land of the black headed people,** which would mean that Adam (interpreted red clay) was a black man. These archaeologists aren't stupid, these people are just sick! Are you trying to tell me that everybody in Mesopotamia was black except Adam, Abraham and Shem? Stop with the foolishness, we have had about as much of the malarkey that we can stand! The cradle of civilization was in Mesopotamia and not in Africa. The next piece of evidence that I will present to support a 6000 year human history is some of the oldest trees found on earth.

METHUSALAH-4,848 YEAR OLD TREE

NATIONAL FORESTS OF CALIFORNIA

The oldest tree found on earth is the Great Basin Bristle Cone Pine at 4848 years (Methuselah).The method of dating trees is simple, each tree ring inside the tree represents 1 year of the trees existence. Now some of you are thinking the earth has to be over 6000 years old because the oldest rock found on earth was dated at 4.2 billion years. I have no problem with the age of the earth because the Bible says that in the beginning God created the heaven and the earth, which would imply that there is no way to put a date on the beginning. In the 2nd chapter of Genesis the Lord talks about the generations of the heavens and the earth, this would suggest that the earth has gone thru cycles. What is the point? The scientists and archaeologists know for a fact that they only have 6000 years of written human history. Prehistoric man is a fabrication of the evolutionists mind; this is their way of filling in the missing gaps. It also means he doesn't have to prove anything that he imagines.

KISH TABLETS 3500 B.C-ASHMOLEAN MUSEUM
THIS OBJECT IS 5500 YEARS OLD

The Kish tablet is a limestone tablet found at Tell al-Uhaymir, Babil Governorate, Iraq the site of the ancient Sumerian city of Kish. A plaster-cast of the artifact is today in the collection of the Ashmolean Museum. The Kish tablet is inscribed with proto cuneiform signs. It has been dated to ca. 3500 BC (middle Uruk period). This is the city State Erech in your King James Bible (Genesis (10:10). I have worked with Egyptian hieroglyphics and a lot of the symbolism on this tablet looks like the hieroglyphics of ancient Egypt to me.

I would like to revisit the conversation concerning Prehistoric man; the time that man recorded nothing. If you believe this I got a lake for sale, even little girls that play hopscotch will draw on the ground and what about the graffiti artist? This man is inclined to draw and write, as witnessed by the cuneiform tablets. The black kings of Mesopotamia and the black kings of Egypt ruled the earth for the first 3400 years of mans existence on earth, this is fact not fiction. The European historians know this is fact because you didn't get white European rulership over the entire earth until 606 B.C with the arrival of Nebuchadnezzar of Babylon. Now Jesus the Christ made a statement in the book of Luke (Luke 21:24) verse 24, they shall fall by the edge of the sword and shall be led away captive into all nations and Jerusalem shall be trodden down of the Gentiles **until the times of the gentiles be fulfilled**. The Lord set a time when Gentile rule would end and on paper and that time occurred in 2004, so right now (theoretically) the Gentiles are ruling on the Lords day. See the book of Isaiah (Isaiah 60:19-22)verse 19, the sun shall be no more thy light by day neither for brightness shall the moon give light unto thee but the Lord shall be unto thee an everlasting light and thy God thy glory. Verse 22 a little one shall become a thousand and a small one a strong nation, **the Lord will hasten it in his time**. You'll need to read the entire 60th chapter of Isaiah to get some understanding; this is referring to the second coming of Christ and I know it to be fact because he talks about Israel coming back into the land and the sun not shining. This will only happen in the day of the Lord. The Gentiles (European nations) rulership will end when black Jesus shows up with the angels and the saints. See Joel the 3rd chapter you'll need to read the entire chapter to see that it's talking about the gathering of Israel (Joel 3:9 & 10). Verse 9, **proclaim you this among the Gentiles prepare war** wake up the mighty men let all the men of war draw near let them come up Verse 10, beat your plowshares into swords and your pruning hooks into spears let the weak say I am strong. Verse 11, **assemble yourselves** and come all ye heathen and gather yourselves together round about thither cause thy mighty ones to come down o Lord. Why is the proclamation aimed at the Gentiles? Because it is written in the book of Matthew (Matthew24: 21 & 22) verse 22 and **if those days had not been shortened no flesh would be saved**, in order for the earth to be freed from the grip of these European nations God must put down their rulership. Also who possesses the weapons of mass destruction on this earth? The **United States, Russia, United Kingdom, China, France and Pakistan**. All of these nations are Gentile nations with the exception of Pakistan. In case you haven't noticed, black Hebrews are spread among all the nations of the world but in order for the Lord to free his people he must go to war with the European powers. The European powers of the earth and her allies will try to go to war with the eternal. This is what Armageddon is all about plus this white man doesn't want to relinquish his grip on the poor of this world. When God shows up the foolish European nations will attempt to hold on to the thing that God loves the most and that is the Hebrew Israelite. God destroyed Egypt because she had the love of God in her bosom. The European powers have destroyed themselves with their treatment of the sons of God over the last 2700 years. The Europeans will attempt to kill God. They think because he allowed himself to be crucified on the cross 2000 years ago that it can be done again. See the book of Psalm **(Psalm 2:1-4)** verse 1, why do the heathen rage and the people imagine a vain thing? Verse 2, the kings of the earth set themselves and the rulers take council together against the Lord and against his anointed. Verse 3, saying let us break their bands asunder **and cast away their cords from us (is this the crystal firmament?).** Verse 4, he that sits in the heavens shall laugh; the Lord shall have them in derision. For all of you who have it in your mind to volunteer for the armed forces **beware that you don't fight against our God and our King**, because if you do you will receive the reward of the wicked, let me show you. In the book of Zachariah **(Zachariah14:12)**verse 12, this shall be the plague wherewith the Lord will smite all the people that have fought against Jerusalem; **their flesh shall consume away while they stand upon their feet and their eyes shall consume away in their holes and their tongue shall consume away in their mouth.** Do we have anything in the history of this man that I could use as a visual aid so you can get an idea what God is going to do to this rebellious man? Yes unfortunately I do, history has recorded images of this cruel European dropping the atomic bomb on the cities of Japan; **Nag**asaki and Hiroshima. The same thing is going to happen to the armies of this Earth when they make war against the Jesus of the Bible! For those of you that know Jesus as a kind and fuzzy guy....it is true and I can't deny it. There's one problem though.... just like we all have a button, that if you push it you will see that other side of us. Our God has another side to himself that he doesn't like to display, case in point the flood. In case you have forgotten he also has prepared a lake of fire for Satan the Devil and his angels. That is his other side.....and believe me...you don't want none of that!

CHAPTER 12   WAR WITH THE GOD OF ISRAEL

Read the book of Revelation (Revelation 19:11-14) verse 11, I saw heaven opened and behold a white horse and he that sat upon him was called faithful and true and in righteousness he doth judge and make war. Verse 12, **his eyes were as a flame of fire**. in the book of Revelation (Revelation 1:14 & 15) verse 14, **his hair was like lamb's wool verse 15, his feet as if burned in a furnace**. When the heaven rolls back like a scroll all of the racist nations on this earth will see a black God. They will have to decide if they can accept black rulership or be damned forever! There is a scene in the book of Revelation (Revelation 19: 13& 15) verse 13, he was clothed with a vesture dipped in blood and **his name is called the word of God** and the armies which were in heaven followed him upon white horses clothed in fine linen white and clean. Verse 15, and out of his mouth goes a sharp sword that with it he should smite the nations; and he shall rule them with a rod of iron. The lord is going to give the rulership of this entire planet to the saints. Run with me to the book of Daniel (Daniel 7:27) verse 27 <u>**and the Kingdom and dominion and the greatness of the Kingdom under the whole** heaven shall be given to the people of the saints of the most High,</u> whose Kingdom is an everlasting Kingdom and all Dominions shall serve and obey him. **Change is on the way and they know it!**

IMAGE OF JESUS WITH THE APOSTLES

CATACOMBS OF DOMITILLA, ROME-4TH CENTURY

The God that will appear on this Earth when the 7th trumpet sounds will be black just like this ancient fresco of Jesus. The United States detonated a nuclear bomb on Hiroshima and Nagasaki**(1945)**in World War II, the heat of the blast was so intense that some of the people were vaporized where they sat. I have some photos of what happened to the Japanese men, women and children on that fateful day. **This is going to one of the saddest things that you have ever seen!**

THE EXPLOSION OF AN ATOM BOMB

KTL TV, LOS ANGELES CALIFORNIA 1951

HIROSHIMA PEACE MEMORIAL- MUSEUM

This baby got caught outside and was scorched to death and appeared to have died an agonizing death!

HIROSHIMA PEACE MEMORIAL- MUSEUM-JAPAN
SHADOWS OF TWO-THREE GIRLS JUMPING ROPE

HIROSHIMA PEACE MEMORIAL- MUSEUM-JAPAN
MAN OR WOMAN WALKING WITH A CANE

HIROSHIMA PEACE MEMORIAL- MUSEUM-JAPAN
CAT SEEKING A MOUSE?

The last thing the two little girls **(possibly three)** will remember is jumping rope and probably the last thing the cat remembered was looking for a mouse….this is pathetic! I tell the young ministers of the Gospel that their first assignment is to deliver themselves from God's wrath and then deliver the people. I'm from the hood and we have a thing in the hood called a drive by, that's where somebody drives down the street in a raggedy car shooting out the windows at someone that they have a problem with. Usually these guys shoot the innocent bystander and that is what will happen to anyone that gets in the Lord's way! The shadow of the two little girls, **possibly three,** the old person and the cat is all that was left of four living beings! They had nothing to do with the war….they were in the way and that is the position that the so-called Negro is in….we are in the way. If a major war broke out today…where would the Negro go? Think about it.

THE CITIES OF THE WORLD

What about the beautiful cities of this World? See Revelation 16:19 and **the cities of the nations fell**. When Jesus came the first time **he came as the Lamb of God** but when he comes back the second time he will be coming back as **the lion of the tribe of Judah.** I have selected **the city Hiroshima** and the **city Hamburg** as examples of what the Earth will look like when the Lord fights the battle of Armageddon.

HIROSHIMA PEACE MEMORIAL MUSEUM, JAPAN

HIROSHIMA DESTROYED

HIROSHIMA PEACE MEMORIAL-MUSEUM-JAPAN
MASS GRAVES OF THE DEAD-HIROSHIMA-1945

HIROSHIMA PEACE MEMORIAL MUSEUM, JAPAN
HIROSHIMA DESTROYED

I placed these images of Hiroshima in this section of this book so that you could get a better understanding of what is on the way. In the book of Jeremiah (Jeremiah 25:31-33) verse 33, **the slain of the Lord shall be at that day from one end of the Earth even unto the other end of the Earth.** Don't believe your minister when he tells you that the Bible is speaking in metaphors, he is lying. If you are reading this book you are blessed because you are getting a sneak preview into the 2nd coming of Jesus the Christ. The destruction of the Gentiles (European powers) coincides with the returning of the Hebrew Israelite (so called Negro) back to Jerusalem. It also means that the native **Indians will get their lands back, the aborigines of Australia will get their land back, the South Africans will get their lands back from the Dutch and the true Egyptian will get his land back from the Turk.** I want to make this very clear the liberation of the so called Negro is actually the liberation of the entire planet. It also means that these Europeans' in America have to go back to North Germany where they originated from. So as you can see, **the Lord never told the black man that he would be in the land of captivity forever** and the liberation of the black man will coincide with the destruction of the European power system as we know it. How will the world receive the news of the European demise? See Ezekiel 35: 14 **"When the whole Earth rejoices I shall make you desolate."** The entire planet shall rejoice at the fall of the European international Monetary Fund **(IMF & WORLD BANK)**, the European colonizers, NATO and the European union.

THE EVERYMAN PROPHECY

In the book of **Leviticus (Leviticus 25:8,9,10,13)**verse 8, thou shall number seven Sabbaths of years unto thee seven times seven years and the space of the seven Sabbaths of years shall be unto thee forty and nine years. Verse 9 then shall thou cause the trumpet of the jubilee to sound on the tenth day of the seventh month in the Day of Atonement, **shall you make the trumpet sound** throughout all your land. Verse 10 and you shall hallow the fiftieth year and proclaim liberty throughout all the land unto all the inhabitants thereof. **It shall be a jubilee unto and you shall return every man unto his possession and you shall return every man unto his family**! Verse 13, **in the year of jubilee you shall return every man unto his possession.** Now check this out; when that trumpet blows in the year of jubilee **every man, not some men, but every man must go back to his family and his land.** The so-called Negro (Hebrew Israelite) is part of **the everyman prophecy**, every man including the Negro in America must return to the land of his father's whether he wants to or not! See **Isaiah 13:10 verse 10, for** the stars of heaven and the constellations thereof shall not give their light, **the sun shall be darkened** in his going forth and the moon shall not cause her light to shine, why? Verse 14, because **everyman (Negro) shall turn to his own people** and flee **everyone into his own land**. You see every man was given a plot of land when the Lord divided to the nations their inheritance (Genesis 10:25) this took place in the year 2243 B.C, in the days of Peleg. I know you have been intoxicated by this Europeans' technology, but believe me when the Lord comes back, the European will flee from you while attempting to flee from God. When this7th trumpet is blown the kingdoms of this world will become the kingdoms of our Christ; the angel of the Lord is referring to this European power structure on the earth right now. **If you stop playing and look at the international arena** you will see that **the former** European **colonizing nations and** European enslaving nations **are to this day attacking nations of color; France, United States, England and the Dutch**. All of these nations have hidden themselves in world organizations with nicknames like **NATO, European Union or the Allies;** these nations have not changed their ideology towards nations of color. Instead of colonizing nations of color they send in the International bankers under the pretense of helping the black nation. The International Monetary Fund and the World Bank operate under the umbrella of globalization and free market. These banking cartels have a formula that destroys the nations that they lend money to. This is how it works; these banks give paper money loans, what's the problem with paper money? It is worthless because it is not backed by silver and gold, they call this Fiat money. The international bankers determine who will lead the country. The loans will come with high interest rates that can never be paid back.....Africa. The G-8 nations get to buy the infrastructure of the borrowing nation...they call it free enterprise but I call it new colonization. The G-8 nations are allowed to dump their goods in your country below market; this drives your business men out of business. To add insult to injury the leader chosen by the international bankers is allowed to flee the country with billions. What are the people left with? When the nation cannot meet the loan requirements the only way to pay the loan back is on the backs of poor people....taxes! Recession and depression is the next order of business and once the people realize the scam that has taken place they revolt. To put down the revolt the international bankers send in the watch dog...the United Nations....the same good old boys! Not only is your country owned by outside investors but you also find yourself occupied! This is what happened to 53 nations in Africa after post colonialism, and unto this day the continent has not repaid back the interest on these loans. This is why the Bible teaches that usury (INTEREST) is a moral crime! It is secret bondage to the lender, they know for a fact that you can never pay the interest back, let alone the principal. Examine America's debt, 90% of her debt is the interest that she is being charged by the Federal Reserve to print money for us. The point that I am trying to make is simple, the only one who can destroy this so-called new World order **(good old boy power structure)** is Jesus.

CHAPTER 13 THE ANSWER TO THE NEGRO QUESTION

Based on **the Images taken from the tombs, D.N.A, artifacts, the Bible, and the secret air lift of Ethiopian Jews; the Negro is none other than the original Jew**. The **law of darkness** was used exclusively against us so that by not reading and doing our own studies we would never come to the knowledge of self. The second question that was raised was his origination; the so called Negro in America did not originate in Africa but had his origination in Mesopotamia, the land of the black headed people. Our father Abraham crossed over from Mesopotamia into Canaan and there our fathers were born, Isaac and Jacob. From Jacobs loins came the 12 tribes and from his 12 sons the whole of Israel. We had colonies in Alexandria, Carthage, Cyrene and Elephantine, **the black Jewish colonies descended into Africa during times of invasions** such as **the Assyrian invasion of 722 B.C, the Babylonian invasion of 609 B.C. We fled into Africa during the Roman destruction of Jerusalem in 70A.D, the Arab invasion in 640 A.D and the destruction of Jerusalem by Hadrian 132 A.D.** It was from these invasions that our fathers situated themselves along the wheat coast, gold coast and slave coasts of Africa; and from here our fathers formed one of the greatest black empires that the west fails to teach black children about, the Ashanti Empire. **Now I shall proceed to trace the Negros lineage from Shem, Luke 3: 23-38, verse 25, which** was the son of Nagge. In Hebrew the word Nagga is Ni##a, which means black in antiquity. This means that one of Jesus relatives was so black that they called him this word. **Luke3:36 verse 36 which was the son of Arphaxad,** which was the son of **Shem** verse 38 which was the son of **Enos**, which was the son of **Seth**, which was the son of **Adam, which was the son of God**! The Negro in the America's are the true sons of God. We trace our lineage thru Shem, not Ham nor Japheth and this has been proven! The title of the book is the Negro Question, who is he and where is he from. **I have attempted to prove to you that the so called Negro in America has his origins in Mesopotamia and from that region of the world came forth black people.** <u>When the Lord became upset with our fathers he deported them not to Africa but he sent them packing back to Mesopotamia</u> from whence they came; <u>First to Assyria of Mesopotamia</u> and <u>secondly to Babylon which was in Mesopotamia.</u> The migration of the black Mesopotamian into Africa is no more a freakish event than the barbarians of Europe migrating from North of Germany to Britain in the 5th century. What then is the solution to the Negro question? **The solution to the Negro question is simple**, the Europeans in America will never respect the achievements of black Americans and they have proven that with their treatment of the Negro President Obama. The Negro has proven his worth to this country, we made them rich, we fought in all of his wars; Civil War, Spanish American War,

Mexican War, WW1,WW2, Grenada, Vietnam , Iraq, Indian wars, Korean War, Gulf War, and in Afghanistan. America's enemies were our enemies even though we have been treated like the dung that the dog leaves in the grass. Counting from the year 1865 to 2019, **in 154 years**, we have caught up to the white American in education, technology, science, politics and athletics; what can we achieve after such a sprint on the universal time line? **The only thing left for this Negro to accomplish is the end game, and that being the formulation of his own nation**. There were 193 nations represented at the United Nations, and there were 162 nations represented that didn't have, **individually,** the population that the Negro in America has and that being **42 million souls**. We have all the skill sets of nationhood, a black President, black generals, scientists, morticians, educators, businessmen and astronauts. It is time for the Negro in America to be seated at the table of nations; **this is the final solution...nationhood!** The European establishment knows that what I write is truth because all Europeans have one thing in common. Europeans want to maintain white rulership; they just differ on the ways to do it. Case in point the Klu Klux Klan vs the Democratic Party or the Tea Party vs the Republican Party. You black folk had thoughts of nostalgia when Obama got elected but guess what? Nothing has changed and what further proof do you need that you need your own nation.

CHAPTER 14   THE WHITE JEWISH QUESTION

I found it quite amusing that I had to gather all of the information that I showed you to prove that the Negro in the America's is the Hebrew Israelite of the Bible. I showed you the replica of the Ark of the Covenant; carbon dated between 700 and 1000 years old. I showed you the images of the black Jews from the tomb of Beni Hassan, I showed you the different airlifts into Jerusalem of the black Ethiopian Jews, I showed you the Sambatyan Jews of Nigeria, I showed you the London Times article of the Ashanti priest crossing the Prah river with Holy to Yahweh on his cap and the breastplate. I showed you the coin with Josephs image on it, I showed you the image of Hagab the Judean archer, I called to your attention the letter the Queen of the Ashanti wrote to the Queen of England telling her that the Ashanti worshipped the God of the Sabbath; I showed you how the Ashanti got there name, that these were the people of Ashan in the bible. **What about the white Jew in Jerusalem? Where is his proof of origination, where are his artifacts, and what exactly did he present to the United Nations in 1948 that they gave him a charter for nationhood and the land of our fathers?** In order to answer that question we must answer **the white Jewish question**, in a very deliberate and forensic scientific type of manner. The white Jewish question begins with a trip backwards in time, to Europe, to a small nation situated near the Black Sea and

Caspian Sea called the Khazars. **The King of the Khazars traces his lineage not thru Shem but thru Japheth** the son of Noah. A letter is written from King Joseph of the Khazars in which he details his people's lineage, **"we have found in the family registers of our fathers."** Joseph asserts boldly that **Togarma**, the son of Japheth (Gentiles) had ten sons and the names of their offspring are as follows: **Uigur, Dursu, Avars, Huns, Basilii, Tarniakh, Khazars, Zagora, Bulgars, Sabir <u>we are the sons of Khazars the seventh</u>! This is an official document from the now deceased Khazar nation stating to the world that we are not from Shem, we are the sons of Japheth**! See the book, the 13th tribe Koestler page 72. These people kept the Russians (Vikings) from invading Arabia and kept the Arabs from invading Europe! The Khazars were a Turkish kingdom that was situated between the Black Sea and the Caspian Sea. The Khazar settlement is mentioned in the Crimea, the Ukraine, Hungary, Poland and Lithuania and **these settlements migrated into Russia and Poland.**

MAP SHOWING LOCATION OF KHAZARS

Listen to me for a moment....**this section of the book is not meant in any form or fashion to produce hate, racism or bias against the European Jews of Israel. We don't have time to hate; we are trying to teach our people the truth!** If you are a teacher, take hate out of your teaching...it gives the Church a black eye! I am simply trying to answer the Jewish question that has become a burning fire in the circles of the wise men! Based on historical correspondence between the Muslim Caliphs and the King of Khazaria it has come to light that the Khazars chose Judaism over Islam and Christianity so as not to be a servant to the Pope or the Caliph. Historically, **the people of Khazar were a Turkish Finnish people that originated in Asia that entered Europe by land route north of the Caspian Sea.** It has been recorded that they settled in Eastern Europe and established the Khazar Kingdom. The Khazar King, Joseph, chose Judaism as the state religion. The Khazar Kingdom collected tribute from at least 25 nations that they conquered; and from these 25 nations, the Khazar King reportedly by force or consent married one of their daughters. It is interesting to note that this kingdom lasted **for 500 years,** yet it is as if these people who converted to Judaism never existed! **The coming of the Rus** or the Russians was the beginning of the end for the Khazar Kingdom. They were defeated by the Russians in the late 10th century A.D. and by the middle of the 13th century the conquest was complete!

This is the point in history where this Kingdom of converted Jews becomes lost in history, but how? You can still find their name on ancient maps and the exact location of their kingdom. How could a nation that held off the feared Vikings and the Arabs of Arabia seemingly become lost in the annals of world history? It is simple, upon being defeated by the Russians, the Khazar people became incorporated into the rising Russian empire! Note**, a large part of the Khazar Jews were concentrated in, Hungary, Crimea, Ukraine, Poland, Lithuanian , Galician , Romania** and other states who in turn were conquered and incorporated into the Russian empire. For a reference, see the Palestine plot; author B. Jensen, pages 2 and 3. The Karites of Poland and Russia are steadfast in that we are the descendants of the Khazar people in this generation! When these people showed up at the United Nations they had no artifacts, and do you know why? Remember these people had their origination in Asia not Mesopotamia and eventually migrated to Europe. The Tarim mummies prove this, the D.N.A, from the 5000 teeth analyzed prove this. We know that Jacob had a twin by the name of Esau, you know him as Edom, the white Jew looks nothing like Jacob or Esau. See the pictures on the next page of an Ancient Israelite, Aristobulus the Edomite and the unknown European Jew. See the next page.

ABRAHAM-DURA EUROPA SYNAGOGUE-SYRIA-IMAGE 3900 YRS OLD

ARISTOBOLUS-ESAU SEED-JEWISH VIRTUAL LIBRARY   **ISHMAEL SON OF ABRAHAM**

LEVITE SINGERS-BRITISH MUSEUM   **JOSEPH-CAIRO MUSEUM-EGYPT**

EUROPEAN JEW-SEED OF JAPHETH

Everyone on this page is the seed of Abraham and they all look the same except this new Jew, the question is simple, what happened?

205

The answer to the white Jewish question is simple, he is not of the seed of Shem not because I don't want him to be; he is not the seed of Abraham because he doesn't look like the ancient artifacts. Based on the statement of King Joseph of Khazar, he is of Togarmah the son of Japhet, the gentile! **The historians trace his origins to Asia and from Asia he ascended into Europe; his resting place is not in Jerusalem but in the region of the Black Sea and the Caspian Sea.** For the sake of argument, I took the images from the tomb of Ben Hassan, a 2300 year old image of Abraham, an image of Joseph from a museum in Egypt, an image of Edom Aristobulus of Chalci, an image of a ancient Arab and an image of a corn rolled Hebrew going into the Assyrian captivity; the unknown Jew didn't look like any of the artifacts. The coin with Aristobulus of Chalcis was used for another reason, it has been stated by some of the elders, of which I hold in high esteem, that these European Jews in Jerusalem are Edomites but if you take a real close look at the coin of Aristobulus he has a big Negro nose, an afro, and the biggest lips I've ever seen. The money is the secret to the true history of this world and this is something that the coin dealers have known for quite some time. These guys that buy ancient coins buy the true history of the nations. The Herodian line is the line of which brother Aristobulus descended from; this was Esau, Jacobs's twin brother. See Genesis (Genesis 25:20-26), verse 21 and Isaac in-treated the Lord for his wife because she was barren and the Lord was in-treated of him and Rebekah his wife conceived. Verse 22 and the children struggled together within her and she said if it be so why am I thus and she went to enquire of the Lord. Verse 23, the Lord said unto her two nations are in thy womb and two manner of people shall be separated from thy bowels. Verse 24,**there were twins in her womb! Verse 25 the elder was called Esau.** Verse 26, the younger was called Jacob. Per the writings of **Flavious Josephus** we find that this **Herod the Great was a descendant of Esau** who was also called Edom, Mt Seir or Idumea. The European Jews that are currently in Israel look nothing like Herod's grandson Aristobulus, so it is of a certainty that the people in the land are not Esau's' seed. The Edomite Aristobulus, looks just like the black Israelites in the image, it is interesting the value humans place on money, the people who will attempt to hide the truth will burn down libraries and important documents but they never burn the money. Now one might say I'm advocating the theory that the Edomite or Idumea is not in the land; t**o the contrary,** history records that the Jews revolted against the Roman Empire in 70 A.D, under Vespasian and Titus Caesar. I found a coin that Vespasian had minted to commemorate his defeat of Judah. See the image on the next page. **Remember <u>we are not interested in hate</u>....we are in pursuit of one thing....the truth.** Hate dilutes the truth and it gives power to those who don't want the masses to hear the truth. Our interest lies in the truth..nothing else!

VESPASIAN COMMEMORATION COIN

JUDEAN COINS 70 A.D

The inscription on the coin reads, "Captive Judah, at its present size this coin simply strikes you as another ancient coin. This coin represents the prophecy that Jesus uttered in Luke that Judah would have a trench placed around her and be carried away captive among the gentiles. It also gives credence to the writings of one maligned Jewish historian, Flavious Josephus; who gave an account of the Roman siege of Jerusalem and wrote that Vespasian was the Caesar at that time. So this coin is an historical artifact, it depicts a time and place in human history. Indulge me for a moment and look at the next page. I've enlarged the reverse side of the coin showing the Hebrew captives, **the man has an afro and a huge Negroid nose;** these are not the features of a European male. See the next page.

SIMON BAR KOKHBA

European males in all of their images depict themselves with straight pointed noses and straight stringy hair. Remember what I told you in previous chapters; the one thing that the Europeans love the most is their money. They will destroy libraries, historical documents, pictures, nations and peoples but never the money. This is their Achilles heel, this is the one reason we have uncovered so much truth about the past. The Romans had been dealing with Judah since the days of Antiochus Epiphany **(215 B.C)**; they knew what we looked like; **Judah Maccabee signed a peace treaty with the Romans in 161 B.C. Vespasian Caesar painted the Jews black because in his generation the Jews were black...am I missing something here? This is the secret of the coin collector they get to see the real history of the World.** The Hebrews (Jews) revolted against the Romans between the years 132-135 A.D and subsequently were crushed by Hadrian Caesar; after the Romans put down the revolt, the Jews were forbidden to enter Jerusalem. It has been recorded that an alien people were permitted to reside in the land of Judah. The next thing that this Hadrian did was **merge** the lands of **Edom, Galilee, Samaria, Judah** and called it **Palestine**. This brought to pass that passage of scripture in the 83rd psalm (Psalm 83:4- 12) Verse 4, they have said," come and let us cut them off from being a nation that the name of Israel may be no more in remembrance. Verse 6, **Edom, the Ishmaelite (Arabs) Moab**. Verse 12, who said let us take to ourselves the houses of God in possession. As these nations did after Nebuchadnezzar destroyed the temple in 587 B.C; so these same nations did after the destruction of Jerusalem by Hadrian in 132 A.D. What did Edom do? He moved into the land and assumed the identity of his brother Jacob. For the sake of visual imagery, I've attached a map for you to see the location of the nations that once surrounded Judah; Ammon, Moab, Arab (Arabs) and Edom. You can see with the close proximity to Judah the ease with which these nations could ascend and descend into Judah. See map and people of Edom on next page. What did the Romans do with the Jews that they captured in 70 A.D? They were sent West across the Mediterranean into Europe as gifts.

By the grace of the Most High God I have been able to provide you with **ancient images of 6 tribes in Israel; this is unprecedented among the modern scribes!** If you look at the image of Edom you can see he looked just like his twin brother Jacob; Judah and Israel. The book of Obadiah states that when Nebuchadnezzar invaded Judah and carried the population

211

captive, the children of Edom entered the land. Read Obadiah chapter 1:10-13, verse 13 you should not have entered into the gate of my people in the day of their calamity, nor laid hands on their substance. The prophet Ezekiel writes practically the same thing, read the 35th chapter of Ezekiel. Finally the identity theft is recorded in the Illustrated Bible Dictionary, part 1 page 411 and part 2 pages, 825 and 826.Those in the know, who don't want you to know the truth, have burned down the libraries **(Julius Caesar burnt the library at Alexandria)** broken the nose on the statues of the black Pharaohs **(Arabs destroyed black statues of the Pharaohs).** Napoleon shot the nose off the Sphinx and King Leopold of Belgium spent 7 days in the Congo destroying government documents. The people who would change history with their lies will go to great lengths to hide the truth. This Aristobulus definitely has an afro, a large Negroid nose and huge lips, not to mention the braids. They have a saying in the streets, **"even Ray Charles can see this.**" Before I leave this section I must note the obvious; based on the physical characteristics of Herods grandchildren one must conclude **that Herod, Philip, Herodias, and Salome of Chalcis** were all black people. In fact the wife of Herod was a **black Maccabean Princess by the name of Miriam**. This is not conjecture ladies and gentleman this is a historical known fact! Unfortunately there aren't any images to produce of this black princess but go back to the chapter where I deal with the color of Israel according to the scriptures. Take a good look at the archaeological evidence, Miriam was a descendant of Judah and was black. I must note that it took me two days of research to try to find additional images of Herod and his offspring but it was fruitless. Most of the coins that had images of his children were so marred that you couldn't distinguish their physical characteristics; the only one worth showing was Aristobulus and his wife Salome. The one thing that continues to astound me is the D.N.A treasure trove in the land of Israel, it has been noted by the esteemed scientists of this generation that the D.N.A safe box is the teeth. I heard one scientist state that people can write anything in a book suggesting their orgins but the D.N.A doesn't lie, it will tell the true tale. To answer the European Jewish question once and for all, why not send a team of scientists to the graveyards of Israel and examine the D.N.A of the ancient Israelites. I can live with the results whatever they may be. I am also confident that Esau is in the land. Based on the historical evidence it has been surmised that he has mingled himself among the Palestinians and is calling himself a black Palestinian Arab. That is the end of the matter concerning the Negro Question, I written to you all that was in my heart concerning this subject. Now I shall proceed to the last pages of this book by revealing the European secret.

CHAPTER 15   THE EUROPEAN SECRET

What is this great secret that the Europeans possess that has been omitted from their history books and that would revolutionize the way the world perceives the so called Negro? What if I told you that the so called Negro was among the first Kings of Europe? The Roman Empire had the distinction of being a multiracial empire. This has been lost on history by the racist reporting by the Europeans in the west, and I shall illustrate this point in a moment. Below is an image of Trajan's column and it clearly shows a group of black men with dreadlocks fighting in the Roman army. **See blown up version on next page.**

Detail from Trajan's Column - Black cavalrymen, allies of the Romans, probably local: absolutely no evidence that they are troops from Africa. The Dacian Wars (101-102, 105-106 A.D.) were two military campaigns fought between the Roman Empire and Dacia during Emperor Trajan's rule. Dacia corresponds to modern countries of Romania and Moldova, as well as smaller parts of Bulgaria, Serbia, Hungary, and Ukraine.

TRAJAN'S COLUMN-ROME

TRAJANS COLUMN-BLACK SOLDIERS DREADLOCKED

Detail from Trajan's Column - Black cavalrymen, allies of the Romans, probably local: absolutely no evidence that they are troops from Africa. The Dacian Wars (101-102, 105-106 A.D.) were two military campaigns fought between the Roman Empire and Dacia during Emperor Trajan's rule. Dacia corresponds to modern countries of Romania and Moldova, as well as smaller parts of Bulgaria, Serbia, Hungary, and Ukraine.

The dread locks can be clearly seen in this ancient snapshot, and the hypothesis is that these brothers were probably part of a contingent from Bulgaria, Serbia, Hungary and the Ukraine. You say this is preposterous, right? Well take a stroll with me thru the Scriptures to a testimony by Paul the Apostle, see Acts 22: verse

24, 25, and 26. Verse 25 and as they bound him with thongs, **Paul said unto the centurion** that stood by, **is it lawful for you to scourge a man that is a Roman and uncondemned?** Verse 26 when the centurion heard that, he went and told the chief captain saying," **take heed what thou doest, for this man is a Roman."** Verse 27 then the chief captain came and said unto him tell me are you a Roman? And Paul said yes. Verse 28 Paul said I was free born! This is the same Paul who was mistaken for an Egyptian and the word Egypt means black. **So, we see here that the Apostle Paul was a black Benjamite Roman citizen,** but let's examine the 2nd chapter of Acts, for there you will see other black Jews come down from Rome on the day of Pentecost. See Acts 2:5 verse 5 and there were dwelling at Jerusalem Jews, devout men out of every nation under heaven. Verse 10 Phrygia and Pamphylia in Egypt and in parts of Libya about Cyrene and **strangers of Rome**, **Jews** and Proselytes. **Did you see that? The Roman Empire consisted of black Roman citizens,** just like you have black Hebrew Israelite American citizens; the Roman Empire had black Jews. The Roman Empire also had Edomites (Herodians) black Arabs, Scots and British. Do you remember what Professor Boyd Dawkins said? The Professor said," **the Black Britain's called themselves Roman citizens."** This is the reason you see dreadlock brothers fighting in Trajan's army. Examine this image of the first black Roman Emperor by the name of Septimus Severus born in Libya or Africa, and became Consul in 190 A.D.

SEPTIMUS SEVERUS ROMAN EMPEROR

WILDWIND COINS

145 A.D-211 A.D

Black Roman Emperor
Pescennius Niger 193 – 194

WILDWIND COINS-ROMAN CAESARS

Doesn't his last name ring a bell for all of you Bible geeks? See Acts 13: verse 1 Now there were in the church that was at Antioch certain prophets and teachers as Barnabas and **Simeon that was called Niger!** He was called **Niger because he was black** and for the same reason the black Jew (so called Negro) in America is called Nig#er. This is not a typing error, I deliberately spelled the word like this so as not to spell the N word! You will not be able to find the Portuguese word Negro on the world maps but you will be able to find the word Niger or Nigeria. This is the region of the world that the Negro in America was stolen from. So the word Nigg## is a misnomer, the true spelling of the word should be Niger. This is a word that denotes where the Negros that were sold in the South came from…not the North. The next image you should be looking at is a German Tapestry found in Germany depicting a black German King being attacked by White barbarians. See the image on the next page.

GERMAN TAPESTERY-WILD MEN AND MOORS

German tapestry 1400 A.D. depicting Black soldiers defending a Black King and Queen (in the windows) from attacking White men. Called by Whites "Wild men and Moors"

GERMAN TAPESTRY-ALL EMPIRES HISTORY FORUM

Take a closer look at the picture, the black king of Germany and his queen are in the castle while their black subjects fight off the barbarian white Germans. The black warriors have on shoes and are riding horses while the barbarians are barefooted, these are the images that are emerging from Europe. Is this not what Professor Boyd Dawkins said? "My fathers were a war like people, not peaceful and they burned and destroyed everything that was British."**Why are you acting surprised?** Benjamin Franklin told you the Germans were a swarthy/black people in his essay; America as a land of opportunity, 1751. **Benjamin Franklin said,"** the Germans are swarthy/black except the Saxons." The Saxons are the European Germans that invaded Europe in 449 A.D. and the whites that we live among in America are their descendants! Benjamin Franklin was 351 years late but at least he knew his history....what about you? **Do you know who you are?** The next image you should be seeing is black Otto the Great, the Emperor of the Holy Roman Empire and his black wife, Edith of England.

OTTO THE GREAT 912 A.D-973 A.D
RULER OF THE HOLY ROMAN EMPIRE
GERMAN RULER

I have let the ancient manuscripts and artifacts speak for themselves, Benjamin Franklin has proven himself to be an upright man. Benjamin Franklin told us that the Germans were a swarthy/black people....but he forgot to tell us how long? The Germans had been a black people eight hundred years before Benjamin Franklin asserted the truth....the Germans are black! This means that the black Germans ruled all of Germany!

**ALESSANDRO DE MEDICI-DUKE OF FLORENCE
FRICK COLLECTION**

This is an image of Alessandro De Medici Duke of Florence, ruler of Florence Italy....not another black ruler! Yes it appears that Benjamin Franklin was correct in his assessment that there were blacks all over Europe. I never heard of this guy before; in high school or college.

THE BLACK COATS OF ARMS-EUROPE

Ad metam

5

Family Crest of: Bower, Bowman, Chatfield, Coults, Fiton, Leader, Miken
(Fairbairn Book of Crests - plate 125)

bower

GERMANBOWER

This first crest that you are viewing was found in Austria Bavaria, as you can see the image portrays a black man with a bow and arrow. In fact, the Scottish name bower was considered the name of an individual or family of bow makers.

GERMAN COAT OF ARMS

13

Family Crest of: Andrewes, Andrews, Collmore, Edington, Gruntham, Mair, Meynell, Moore, More, St. Loe, Weldone, Wittewrong, Wootton
(Fairbairn Book of Crests - plate 135)

German Arms
The Ancient Arms of
More

THE GERMAN- MORE MEANS BLACK

This black coat of arms was initially found in the Austria. This black coat of arms hence is a relic of the Austrian Empire and again, we find among the German speaking peoples the presence of black nobility.

223

FRENCH COAT OF ARMS

13

Family Crest of: Andrew, Andrewes, Andrews, Annyslay, Blaikie, Borthwick, Du Halgoet, Fondre, Gosselin, M'Clelland, Macklellan, M'Lellan, Moir, More, Newborough, Norton, Pecksall, Pexall, Quadering, Seymour, Shirley, Stirling, Weltden
(Fairbairn Book of Crests - plate 134)

French Arms
The Ancient Arms of
More

FRENCH MORE MEANS BLACK

This crest was found in France and upon further research, it has been determined that the black family who owned this crest had a place of honor from ancient times.

SCOTTISH COATS OF ARMS

Andros Family Crest
(Entry from Fairbairn's Book of Crests, 1905 ed.)

Victrix fortuna sapientia

andros

SCOTLAND ANDROS

This black coat of arms as you probably know was found in Scotland Europe, the story that these images tell is simple, the Negro had power in Mesopotamia, Africa and in Europe. In fact the black man obtained power where ever the sole of his foot tread upon. Andrew, Chief of the clan, rendered homage to King Edward I of England in1296.

SPANISH COATS OF ARMS

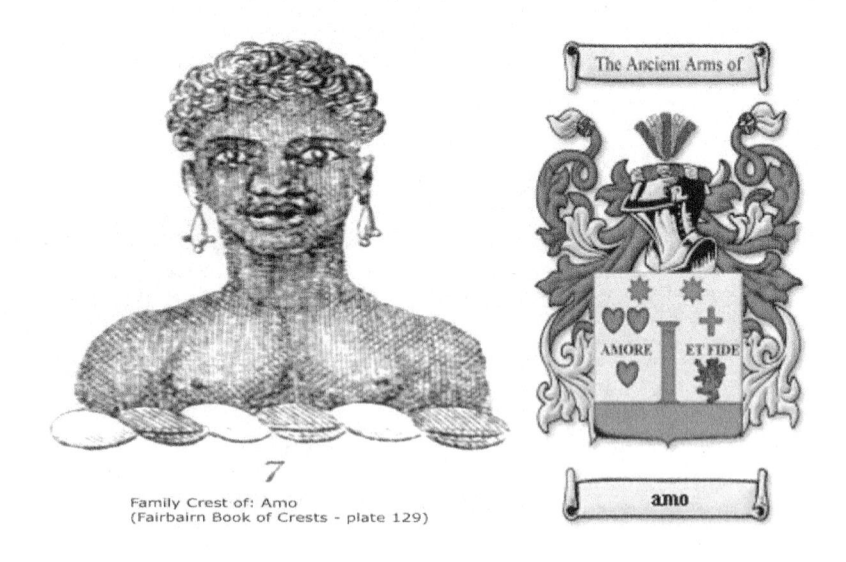

Family Crest of: Amo
(Fairbairn Book of Crests - plate 129)

amo

SPANISH AMO

This black coat of arms was found in Spain, this the historians cannot deny. For it is still fresh in the minds of the European historian, concerning the black Moors who ruled Spain. How did all of these black men and women get to Europe before the slave trade? These uninformed generations of historian's seem to conveniently forget one historical fact, and that fact is the Romans were a multiracial Empire. They ruled the known world, white black, red, and orange, it didn't matter to them. Within the empire there were black Kings as long as they paid homage to the Romans. Another fact missed by the historians of this generation, is that Roman Britain was inhabited by Roman citizens before the Angles and Saxons invaded the country by ship. The inhabitants of Roman Britain were a mixture of freed men and women some

226

black and some white. **In the Roman Empire all whites were not free men as one would suppose.** My mind goes back to the Apostle Paul's conversation with the Roman Centurion in Acts the 22nd chapter verse 27,28. Verse 27 reads then the chief captain came and said unto him, tell me, art thou a Roman? He said yea. Verse 28 and the chief captain answered, with a great sum obtained I this freedom. And Paul said, but I was free born, this is the same Paul the Centurion in previous chapters mistook for an Egyptian (Egypt means black). Here is the testimony of a black Jew born as a free Roman citizen. This is the problem that I have with this modern historian, either his vision is blurred or he has no interest in the truth. This modern historian makes the boast that he has attended and graduated from some of the most prestigious Universities in America, but the history that they report is amateurish and unfounded! Now I would be lying if I tried to tell you that black people ruled all of Europe because I can't produce the evidence to substantiate that claim. But I can tell you this with great clarity, this negative image of the Negro as a slave and a servant is an invention of the United States and it is not the true image of the so called Negro.

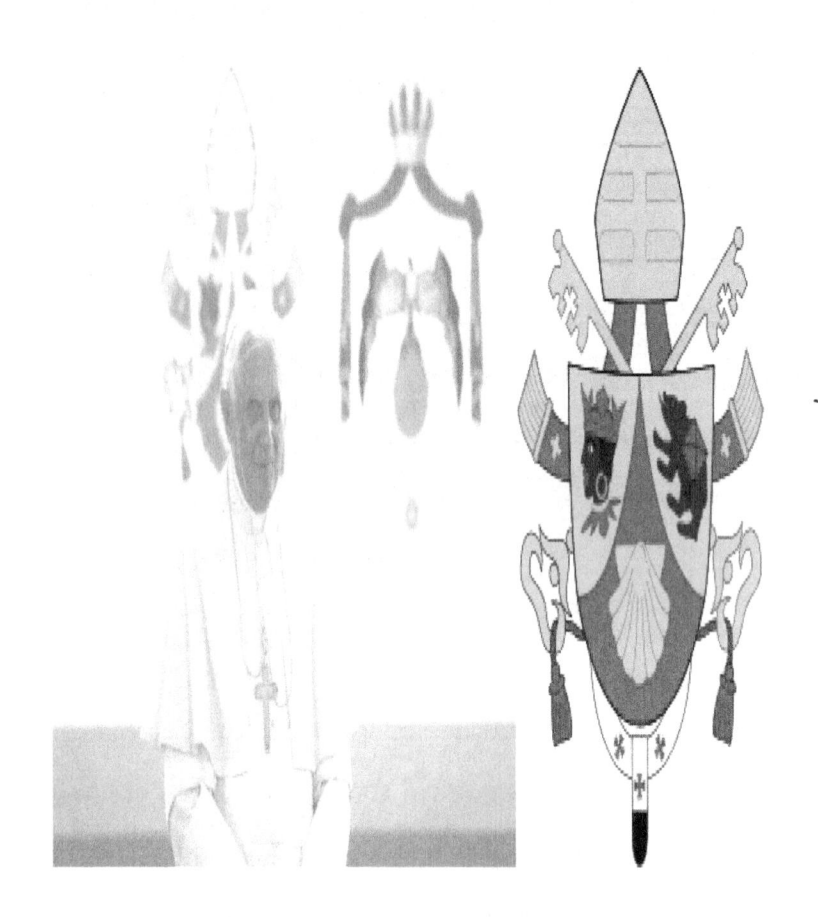

**POPE BENEDICT WITH HIS BLACK
GERMAN COAT OF ARMS!**

I knew that I would have to show you something shocking to make you see the light, so I present to you **Pope Benedict with his black German coat of arms.** The coat of arms to the left of the Pope is the same coat of arms in his background. **This is the coat of arms that this current Pope wears and it is indisputable evidence of the former status of black people in Europe!**

CONCLUSION

I thought within myself wow, how do you end a book with all of the information that was given to the reader? What could I say that would equal the sensation of the books contents? The first thought that came to my mind was the wisdom of God, how he hid the **truth in the Tombs of the Pharaoh's, on the faces of ancient coins, on statues, on coats of arms, in the historical records of nations themselves, but mostly how God preserved 6000 years of human history in the greatest history book of them all, the Holy Scriptures!** What have I actually done in writing this book? Have I come up with new knowledge, has some new wisdom crept into my mind not so, the only thing that I have done, is what our fathers instructed each and every one of us to do and that is to question all things. People give credit to the Greek philosopher Socrates when they quote the phrase", **man know thyself"**, I am of the opinion that this is God's statement to the inhabitants of the earth, to all nations , peoples, black, white, red, yellow whatever the color of your skin, wake up from your mental slumber and remember who you are. Take the time out of your busy lives and check the record of the past. Examine what occurred before you were born because as the wise King Solomon said" **who can see what will come after him**". **In 1929 the Vatican question was answered with the passing of the Lateran treaty creating Vatican City** and giving complete sovereignty to the Papacy. **In 1948 the Jewish question was answered when the United Nations gave the European Jews the land of Judah. The Iraqi question was answered with the assassination of Saddam Hussein and his sons. The Libyan question was answered with the invasion of Libya and the subsequent assassination of Gaddafi.The Sudan question was answered** with the country being split into two countries, but **the Negro question has never been answered.** One of the reasons the Negro question has not been answered, is because the artifacts and images have been purposely withheld from the Negro community or painted over. The second reason the Negro question went unanswered is because we allowed our enemies to teach us world history, but the history we were taught was Euro world or this modern Europeans version of the past. Unto this very day our sons and daughters are being taught an erroneous education handed down by the system. The time of our departure is at hand, the King of the universe is on his way back to set the earth back in order. The time that the Most High has set for the rulership of the Gentiles has come to an end. The liberation of the son's of God and the poor of this planet is upon us all, God bless you and make sure you recommend this book to someone else, Peace!

THE NEGRO ACT!!

Repeat after me! I am obligated after reading this book to tell somebody in my church, grammar school, high school or college about it. I am obligated to give this book to my pastor and my deacons; I am obligated to have this book sitting in my house on the coffee table with my bible; for it is a treasure within itself. This is the thing that the Europeans fear the most and that is the reverse brainwashing of the Negro in America.

Jesus said" You shall know the truth and the truth shall set you free".

GO IN PEACE FOR YOU ARE FREE!!

CONTACT THE AUTHOR

Lee0260@comcast.net

Printed in Great Britain
by Amazon

17539142R00132